BACKPACK BLUES

AF207398

Ignite

The Fire Within

MELODY DEAN DIMICK

CONTENTS

Part I: Backpack Blues

Part II: Ignite the Fire Within

Backpack Blues, 2018
ISBN: 978-1-943789-83-2

Cover design and layout by: WhiteRabbitgraphix.com

This is a work of fiction. Any characters, names and incidents appearing in this work are entirely fictitious. Any resemblance to real persons, living or dead, is purely coincidental.

This book may be purchased through

Amazon.com and Amazon Kindle;
Taylor and Seale Publishing.com
www.taylorandsealeeducation.com
Barnes and Noble
Books-A-Million

Taylor and Seale Publishing, LLC. Daytona Beach, Florida 32118
Phone: 1-386-760-8987
www.taylorandseale.com

Dedication

Backpack Blues was inspired by and is dedicated to
my former students.

ACKNOWLEDGMENTS

The author would like to thank the following people for their contributions to this book:

My husband, Barry Dimick, read and listened to every poem and revision. He also made the coffee to get my creative juices flowing. My college suitemates, Marie Winager Ginter and Sharon Stanley Champine, read and encouraged me through many drafts. The Village Café Writers gave editorial comments and encouragement. My writing coach, Joyce Sweeney, provided excellent advice on the poetry section, prepublication. My copy editor, Beth Mansbridge, edited Part II, prepublication. Mary Custureri, Ed.D, believed in me, gave me advice, and published two of my books.

A special thank-you to: Taylor and Seale Publishing's editor and Volusia County, Florida, poet laureate Dr. David B. Axelrod, who made editing suggestions; my parents, who taught me the importance of an education and bought my first books; and my son, Barry, and his wife, Krista, who encouraged me.

Finally, I wish to acknowledge the students of Northern Adirondack Central School, DeLand High School, and Lighthouse Christian Academy, who served as the inspiration for the persona poems.

Your poems belong to you.
Hone them, but own them.

Melody Dean Dimick

ADVANCE PRAISE FOR

BACKPACK BLUES

"This important collection by Melody Dimick contains poems adept at juxtaposing the experiences of youth with a steadily encroaching world of increasingly adult consequences. It is at once elegy and anthem. In addition, the work contains very helpful hints on Poetry Slam. As coordinator of MainStreet Art & Culture Slam (one of only four certified slams in the entire state of Florida and only about one hundred worldwide) it is refreshing to find a book that can help those unacquainted with performance poetry make an easier transition from page to stage. I would call it a must read for anyone, but especially young people."

Kevin "Noir Jente" Campbell
Slam Coordinator
Florida State Poets Association
Slam Director
Creative Happiness Institute

"Melody Dimick's *Backpack Blues* presents realistic, unflinching portraits of today's teens. A must read for teens and adults, these powerful poems are sure to provoke thought and dialogue."

Elizabeth Weiss Vollstadt
Author of *Pairs on Ice*

"I can't wait to see you in person! I think you're an extraordinary author, and I can't wait to read all of your books."

Karol Aspiolea
student

PART I

BACKPACK BLUES

MARISOL GARCIA

This is our letter to the world.
Thanks, Emily Dickinson, for
giving Mrs. Deyon the idea to push
us to write our Mountain Valley High anthology.

We acknowledge Edgar Lee Masters,
whose *Spoon River Anthology* knocked
our socks off, inspiring us to voice our truths.

You'll see there was no holding back
in this showcase of our senior year—
we've opened our backpacks
for your inspection. Listen

as we share our world—
a shimmering magical snow globe—
if you will—a transparent ball—
but, at times, a whiteout in a blizzard.

ACE JACKSON

You call me the knave of hearts,
but listen to my gossip.
Foul rumors spread like tumors.

YSABEL GOMEZ

I do not wonder
if I should skip school.
My parents rise at four, trying
to get a head start on the day's earnings.
I watch their efforts to arrive at the fields early,
before the yellow sun sneaks over the skyline.

Despite the scorching heat,
Mom wears worn, worked-out
denim pants, and covers
her arms with a long-sleeved shirt,
the lines on her wrist—
indelible. I sense her pain
as she tries to hide
her bracelet of wounds.

I agonize over the 200 rubber bands
she dons daily.

When tempted to miss school,
I close my eyes and imagine Mom
removing one rubber band from her wrist.
She wraps it around a bundle of ferns
as clippers carve calluses on her other hand.

Yards ahead,
Dad's thirsting, tired skin
sags, oppressed by the
erosion of his America.

He works for me.
"Study hard," he tells me
as we stream north in fall.

In the new school, I notice Mercedes Goldman
wears gold bangles to hide her not-so-secret
scars. I wonder if she'd cut herself if she
saw the purple lines on Mother's wrists.

But I do not wonder
if I should skip school.

I do not wonder.

MERCEDES GOLDMAN

Most days, I'm an Emily Dickinson poem.
You know, the one beginning,
"I'm nobody; who are you?"
Today, I'm a curiosity like Bigfoot.
My friends and I wore cosplay costumes.

Faculty members misunderstood our intent,
threatened expulsion, and freaked corporate Mom.
"How could you jeopardize your college plans?"
She says I must stop living in a fantasy world.

How little she knows about me.
I want to be an animator in my invented world.
Residing in my made-up world
I'll be spared from Wall Street woes,
bankruptcies, and job losses.

Manga comic-book pages beckon.
But Mom doesn't care.
She doesn't recognize goals I hold.
I must fit her chosen mold.

No sense arguing with her.
The disappointment in her eyes,
the contempt in my father's frown
tell me my words fall on deaf ears.

I see my pain in Willow's eyes,
and disgust in Ysabel's stares.
Relief will come tonight.
One slash from my razor, and
emotions drip red from my wrists.

WILLOW PISANO

Pain
Slit
Abuse
Rejection
I recall each wound
A bangle of tears mars my wrist

ACE JACKSON

Don't bet your bottom dollar.
No one escapes from high school.
Don't even bother trying.

CORA SIMMONS

I hear your whispers,
"Hick, trailer trash, redneck,"
so I put my head down
as I look for a seat on the yellow bus.
This seat's saved,
Stormi's glare says.
Her backpack smacks on the seat.

Two words painted in red drip
and shout from the side of our shining
trailer home—NO TRESPASSING.
Don't bother us; we're armed—
our trailer screams, offends,
and angers, isolating me.

Down the narrow aisle,
trying to squeeze into
any spot, I hear "No trespassing,"
from a big mouth begging for a laugh,
and the snicker of another.

I cringe, face warm
and tomato-red, and sneak
a glance back at our tin-can home
with its barbed-wire fence.

As I slide into a seat near Noel,
the other loner, I wonder, was
my survivalist Dad ever normal?
Is he paranoid because of a shared gene,
or as a result of battlefield trauma?

Later, in gym class,
I stand on the sideline, shifting
my weight from foot to foot
and stare at my sneakers.
Weed spreading like poison ivy,
as wanted by team captains
as an irritating rash. I pray
not to be the last chosen, knowing,
to them I'm trailer girl—
too invisible to include.

NOAH NEWMAN

Siri talks back.
Unlike the girl in calculus class,
she answers my questions.

She reminds me when assignments are due.
She places my phone calls.
She tells me the weather so
I know enough to wear a coat.

She doesn't care that I'm a computer whiz.
Thanks, Dad, for the personal assistant.
She was the perfect Christmas gift.

Unfortunately, Mrs. Deyon has said,
"Cell phones are not allowed in class,"
so I've turned Siri off.

Reluctantly, I must admit,
she's not the first girl
I've turned off.

LANGDON CROSS

I would like to say,
Lunch Lady,
I can tell you see past my front,
in the same way I'm aware of
the brown old-age spots
through the gloves you wear.

You know I pretend to have
a home-cooked meal
waiting when I get home,
but you can see hunger in my eyes.

You know I haven't eaten
since this time yesterday,
and you give me a double slice of pizza
and an extra brownie.

Others look at you as if you're
part of the cafeteria,
but to me
you're a lifeline in a white apron,
wearing a hairnet
and transparent gloves.

The only two words you hear
from me are *Thank you,* but
I'm sure you read the full
meaning in my wary eyes.

ACE JACKSON

Father, the king of diamonds
until he drew twenty-two.
Tore the queen right through her heart.

ROSS PARROTTE

After-school football practice
Off to work
Tweeting
Texting
Wii
Facebook
Sexting
Sorry, no time for homework.
Let Marisol eat the brownie points.
I say, "Like whatev."
Maybe, tomorrow
I'll hand it in late.

LEAH JONES

I'm a foster child—a hopeless stray.

I sit in solitude in the cafeteria,
head buried in a borrowed book.

All I want is to eat lunch
without jeers about my fat body.
I'm a foster child—a feral intruder.

Ross appears out of nowhere
like a mid-month pimple.
"Wanna be one of my faves?"
he taunts. "You could sext me a picture
of that great bod."

*What have I done to make
you pick on me?* I could ask
Mr. Football Quarterback,
but I don't.

Somehow, he assumes
I do not get his mocking tone,
but I do. Mrs. Deyon taught us
about sarcasm.

I get up, lick my wounds,
and slink away like the cat in Sandburg's
"Fog" without finishing the soup or the surplus
pizza stuck to the faded, lime-green tray.

I'm a foster child—a hopeless stray.
But have no fear.
I'll soon be on my way.
Graduation's on the horizon—hurray!

JANE DOVE

Hail pelts against my weighty backpack.
In the cloudy night, I'm just another runaway
seeking shelter in a garage, tasting my salty tears.
I'm a rabbit nibbling my trembling bottom lip,
unaware that lurking near the door, the dark-eyed predator
recognizes my distress and deduces I'm hungry for love.

Plain, petite girl escaped the orphanage looking for love,
clutching all my possessions in my worn backpack.
While I consider my options, the scar-faced predator
approaches and sizes me up as an unsuspecting runaway.
Guess he notices me nibbling my now-bleeding bottom lip,
because he offers a handkerchief to wipe away blood and tears.

"Beautiful green-eyes shouldn't shed tears."
His false smile's a carrot in the snare because I seek love.
Like a rabbit, I'm prey, nibbling my quaking bottom lip.
I shiver, and tug on my full backpack …
stare at the purple bruise that forced me to run away.
Slowly, I creep toward the trap of the grinning predator.

"Got a place to go tonight?" asks the predator.
Once again, my olive-drab eyes glisten with tears,
hating that he's pegged me as a runaway.
I pull back—afraid he won't offer love.
"So, Jane, what you got in the backpack?"
He's a satisfied cat licking his top lip.

My eyebrows furrow as soon as my name leaks from his lips.
"How did you know my name?" I ask the predator.
He stares and points to masking tape on my backpack.
Four eyes focus on my tacky label, bringing laughter despite tears.
Like Rapunzel, I let my hair down, vainly seeking fairy-tale love
and a chance to see the world, but despite being an innocent runaway,

I pull back, alarmed at the letters, P-A-Y-N-E. Run away,
my instincts tell me when I read his plate, and I bite my lip.
I doubt the man is a Samaritan motivated by love
when he steers me toward his rusty van, but the predator
pounces, and I'm soon bound, shedding tears.
Payne seizes my only possession—the backpack.

"Nothing's free." He opens my backpack, but I can't run away.
My warm tears taste salty as they reach my quivering lip.
"I'm gonna sell you."
The predator smiles, but offers no love.

PAIGE HACKER

Splatters drip from Jackson Pollock brushes.
My words spit from my public pen.
I shriek sentences.

Get those words right.
Say what I mean.
Show. Don't tell.
My verses rap and rock.
Dance on the page like Derek Hough.

Thin, colorful lines trickle
from Native sand paintings,
but not from my ballpoint.

Tapping the keys on my laptop
re-creates the rhythms of life.
Don't care about Kim and Kanye
or a public feud with Taylor. From within,
my words surface like a mountain spring.

Soon my top-secret, scandalous words will
expose skeletons in faculty closets.
So be it—necessary truths bleed.

I saw something that just wasn't right.
Check out my column in the school paper.

I'm not pulling pages from Peggy
McIntosh's knapsack. I'm not THAT white girl,
but I'm like Katy Perry.
"You're gonna hear me roar."
I saw something the night it hailed.

SAWYAH TRUMAN

Mrs. Deyon assumes she's the only one
privy to sneaky truths of school society,
but crumpled up in wastebaskets
I empty after most go home
are pages other kids find
too painful to let slip—
more secrets than they dare divulge,
but I read words they toss.

I feed trash cans with liquor bottles
gathered from more than students' stashes.
I mop but cannot wash away
pain after a late-night board meeting
rendezvous, but my after-school job
is not to warn. Besides, I need this work

to keep food on the family
table. I know enough to recognize
more goes on in the darkroom
than will be exposed on film
by the photography teacher,
or by me. Two blind parents,
but I see.

I clean toilets, but can't
remove the shame
when I paint over
love, hate, and dishonor
my classmates
scratched on stall doors.

PAIGE HACKER

Missing! Amber alert! Green-eyed Jane Dove is missing.
Caregivers from the orphanage say
the black-haired girl with red-dye streaks on the sides
took off on Saturday night.

Caregivers from the orphanage say,
but I saw her dragged into a rusty van.
Took off on Saturday night?
Grabbed by a creep.

But I saw her dragged into a rusty van.
The black-haired girl with red-dye streaks on the sides,
grabbed by a creep.
Missing! Amber alert! Jane Dove is missing.

SNOW DRIFT

Like my name,
my heart's icy cold.
I'm as wanted as
a March blizzard.

My mother thought she was clever.
Was she under the influence of too much ether?
"Let's call our child Snow," she said.

But our last name is Drift!
I'd have said if I could've spoken.

Rumor says Mom once sat in a stylist's chair
and told of her decision to name me Snow.
Mrs. Deyon, the English teacher, overheard and asked,
"Whatever possessed you to pin
a target on your kid's back?"

Clueless mother had no reply.
As for me, I spend half my day
in the principal's office because
I'm sick of the bully's jokes
and won't be intimidated anymore.
Instead of a reply or tear,
I deliver a fistful of fury.

As soon as the law allows it,
I'll quit school
and marry the first man who proposes—
if his last name isn't
White!
I won't live a fairy-tale life,
'cause my mom's a clueless joker.

WINONA CAMPBELL

Well, Snow, you're right.
What's in a name counts.
Native Americans choose names wisely.

If you were Native American like me, you
wouldn't be stuck with a name you hate.
Our names change to reflect
milestones, accomplishments, and actions.

Members of the tribe moving, flowing
like a river spreading to the ocean, change much.

American pet names and nicknames
are pale shadows, reminding of past
relationships and selves. Some of our names
encourage us to grow and change.

Snow, you would not be teased in our culture.
You're a gift drawn by nature.

ACE JACKSON

Dad played poker and blackjack.
That's how he won the money
for Mother's gold wedding band.

STORMI STARR STEVENS

Say what?

I overheard Snow Drift
complaining to Mrs. Deyon.
Snow says her name
causes her dysfunction.
Here I am in the same classroom.
Every time the teacher calls roll,
I sound like an alliterative weather report.
But do I lash out when kids giggle
after hearing my name?

Have I whined because
insecure bullies tease me?
No way! Get out!
Snow needs to get a grip.

I just flounce my dress and
flip my blonde ponytail.
I know I am the life of every party.

One of those guys will soon
grovel for a date,
and on a whim,
I might grant him one,
or I might not!

Whatever!
I'm as predictable as the—
well, you know the old cliché—
I'm in control,
not my name!

As for bullies,
the key to dealing with them
is to treat them like
a three-day-old tuna sandwich
left in some slob's stinky locker!

MONTEL WELLS

Stormi Starr Seasons just strutted
past me in a Lancôme cloud of Hypnosis,
wearing a hot pink dress.

Well, let me tell you—
she's fine!
She knows how to sell it!

So, I say,
"Stormi, who you going to the prom with?"

"Haven't decided," she says,
"but it sure won't be you!
So, rest your eyes!"

Snap! That sister is so Hollister!

I saw what Paige saw,
but I stay away from the law.
If you see Jane, you're looking at a zombie.

When I'm alone in our dark house,
refrigerator noises jar my psyche.
What's that rattle in the kitchen?
Is there an intruder lurking?

Or are ice cubes falling into the bin?
I sit on the couch, trying to summon
courage to check, but what if
a shady someone is skulking?

Mother says she knows every
groan the house emits.
Well, good for her, but I lie in fear.
Shadows flash on the wall!

Was that a light from a passing car
or a prowler with a flashlight?
Refrigerator noises jar my psyche.
Is my imagination running wild,

or am I in looming danger?
What menace is around the corner?
Is it the creepy guy I met on the internet?
What can I do?

I run to the bedroom
and pull the blanket over my head.
Then, I hear a noise and wonder
what's under my bed.

"Meow!" Out comes my cat, Slumber.

TRAVIS INDIGO

Well, woke up this mornin', had no clue.
Just a po' boy, I'm feelin' blue.
Woke up with Pal asleep by me.
Never realized how lonesome I could be.

Without Pal.

Took my dog Pal for a walk n' a talk.
He chased a groovy cat stalkin' a hawk.
A blue Chevy truck—it crushed him flat.
Took off squealin', 'n' man, that was that.

Well, I miss my Pal,
But what can I do?
Gotta get my head together
'Cause I'm feelin' so blue.

I miss him so bad.
I'm feelin' so sad.
My Pal went away,
And I miss what I had.

Evenin' time, baby, can't see straight.
Evenin' time, doin' homework late!
Supposed to write my lyrics tight!
Singin' the blues, but baby, just can't write.

Can't get the rhythm or the beat!
Without my dog, Pal, by my feet,
My mind's as empty as my bed.
My mind's not workin' since my dog's got dead.

Well, I miss my Pal,
But what can I do?
Gotta get my head together
'Cause I'm feelin' so blue.

I miss him so bad.
I'm feelin' so sad.
My Pal went away,
and I miss what I had.

I don't suck up to no one, so
this poem's not one of those
limericks or quatrains or rondeaus.
But I've got my share of pain and loss.
We read poems with talk
of misery and hope drying like some kind of grape.
Well, Mrs. Deyon, I tell my friends:
Time to *reach*, not shrivel! I say,
stretch an arm toward the sky
like the lady in the harbor.
If your life isn't right, fix it!
Black lives matter. Trayvon mattered.
Stand up to haters dripping with bigotry.
Who we wait-in' for?
Superman? Wonder Woman?
C'mon, get real! No one's gonna
fight our battles for us!
No more weeping like
Gram's lemon meringue pie.
We've gotta be strong
like her black coffee.
I don't like what I see, so
I'm gonna stand my ground—
get up and change it, or if need be,
I'll sit down like Rosa did.
But I'm not waitin' for somebody
to swoop down to rescue me!
You say, don't expect life
to be fair. Maybe, but
I WON'T drink the hater-ade.
When life gets tough,
I don't need someone
else to dry my tears
and make hurt right.
I'm sweating my own sweat!
Hey! I'm not speakin'
from a Trump penthouse apartment—
I'm beat to my socks,
yet I'm still pushing.
I'm not quitting.
It takes work, not sobs
to realize dreams.

SAPPHIRE WASHINGTON

Cancer slowly stole
my mother,
left me to depend on Grandma.
Six months later—
a heart attack took Grandma,
left me in the care of Aunt Autianna
and my occasional dad.
Now I live
in a virtual world,
zooming in and zoning out.
Tweeting,
spending my day texting
on my cell
before, during, and after classes,
multitasking, so I don't have to think.
Don't want downtime
to wonder, is my dad next?
Won't get close to another soul.
Sorry if you think I have 'tude.
If you had the hand I've been dealt,
would you be trusting?
I think not!
You'd probably be dealin'.
Poems are tears that need to be written.
So, don't go all superior on me, Stormi.

ACE JACKSON

Travis lost his dog named Pal.

Dad lost our home the same night.

Sapphire lost way more—face down.

CROSBY BURNEY

A boatload of weird kids attend
this school, but none
weirder than Ace Jackson,
whose father gambled away
his business, his home, and
the family's honor at the table,
leaving Ace to go around
school and town mumbling
twenty-one-syllable asides.

Poor Ace, stuck with a name
his father tied on him
when he was on a lucky streak.

Then his dad's luck ran out
at the blackjack table.

My father's luck ran out
on a battlefield, far away.

In the game of life,
we play against the dealer
until he says, "Game's over."

TERRY BILLINGS

Politicians talk of the cost of war
and money jingles from their lips,
but I lie in my bed late at night
listening to my mother's anguished sobs.

I can tell you right now
a flag folded into a triangle
will never replace her firstborn,
and try as I might to please her,
I can never fill the void.

Drained tormented father, seemingly stoic,
shocked into sad silence ...
broken hearts at home.

Pitying stares from my teachers.
Trophies
collecting dust in the school display case.
Memories of promises unfulfilled.
Talent—
wasted.

Girlfriend left to hug a stuffed bear
Bill won for her at the county fair.

Pundits discuss the price we pay for freedom ...
Well, I've an answer
prodigious:
my brother, Bill, and Crosby's dad.

Why can't we ever talk of peace?
Ka-ching! Ka-ching! Ka-ching!

DIEGO VASQUEZ

Where have you been all afternoon? Myra texts me.
Shooting hoops with Del, I text back.
I went to Zumba workout class, she replies.
And I hate to ask her what Zumba is, but I do.
Diego, are you living in a closet? Call me! she texts.

I do.
I can tell by her voice she thinks I'm in my own world.
I don't admit that I've been in a fog since Dad left.
But I know she knows—everybody does.
"Am I unpatriotic to want this war to end?" I ask her.

Myra takes me out of my private world with her answer.
"No, you're human," she says,
and she adds, "Zumba's my Latin music workout."

"I know I haven't been the most attentive boyfriend lately,
so, want to go shopping at the mall or take in a movie?"

"Shopping!" she says.

And I say, "I'll be over in five to pick you up."
But I feel guilty having fun while Dad's eating
dust, deployed for a third tour of duty,
trying to make my world safe.

Myra surprises me when she says,
"I know about Terry's brother
and Crosby's dad, and I'm scared, too.

LYDIA PERKINS

Divorce.
Overheard word—
like a glacier, froze me,
chilled my core.

Dad hurling angry insults like
stones, slurring, and spitting.
"It's over," he says.

In Mom's face—disgust.
Their differences—
a chasm too wide
to leap.

Both threatening
to take custody of
Todd—
prized possession—
only son—
goes with the business
to be claimed
by the winner of their fight,
spilling our blood ....

Cascading tears tumble in open court.

Passed over—small as
the last leaf on the elm—
how I felt when no one
fought to keep me—
the leftover on the plate.

Just a girl in Dad's
intoxicated world.

Over—
conflicts and snubs meaningless now.

Dad,
dead in a ditch
clutching an empty
bottle of Jack Daniel's
like a lover.

AL MOTT

Don't assume you know me
when you look into my eyes.
Don't jump to conclusions,
I am not what you see!

I don't love sushi and rice!
I like burgers and fries!
My mom is not a tiger mom.
My sister would not be a perfect mate.

She's as independent as a Siamese cat!
Don't mess with her!
Your stereotypes have got to go.
I'm melting into the so-called pot!

I'm me and me alone!
I don't represent a race—
don't call me the Asian kid.
I have a name,

and it's not hard to learn.
No need to speak a foreign language to say *Al!*
Don't assume you know me
until you've made the effort

to say, "'Sup?"
when we study each other at our lockers.

CASSIE SPOTZ

Censored
Deleted
Edited
That's how I feel when I comment.

Forbidden
Blocked
Denied
That's how I feel when I ask to join.

Rejected
Cut
Erased
That's how I feel since I've been dumped.

Bleeped
Excluded
Reduced
That's how I feel right now.

Hungry
Fat
Stressed
That's why I binge and purge.

Alienated
Isolated
Neurotic
OMG! Not that!

TASHAWNA BROWN

I hear your foghorn voice, Teach.
Why can't ya learn to say my name?
You think I rebel when you give me homework,
and that's why I don't do it?
You think I sleep in class because I'm bored?

Well, Mrs. Deyon, let me tell ya.
You don't know the real me!
You have no idea what my "home" is.
You won't call my mother to tell her
I snore in class.
She can't get phone calls in her prison cell.

When you're home sleeping in your bed,
I am working one of my two after-school jobs.
My drug-addict mom has left me.
My sister and brother depend on me now.
As my friend Maya says, "That's how she rolls."

My father doesn't even know I exist.
Who is he? I've wondered.
A neighbor has temporarily taken us in,
but her funds are dwindling.

Fear of the truant officer keeps me in school,
but I have to admit, it's cathartic to write this poetry.
(Yes, I did pay attention and take notes
on all those silly words!)
You wrote that you think my poetry is *poignant*.

Well, I looked that word up.
What's moving to you is my life story!
But so far, it has not been one of romance.
I have no love story.

My whole life's been a blues song!
Guys I meet want
what I'm not giving.
And I've no reason to expect
a happily-ever-after ending.

You say you want me to start
using similes and metaphors?
Highfalutin' words, I can't eat.
My world calls for street-smart toughness.

I am a broken wheel.
My control is rolling, rolling, rolling—
and wobbling away!
I gotta put on the brakes.

And you, Teach, you've
gotta learn to say my name,
even if I whisper when I speak.

ETHAN STAFFORD

This is just to say I think
that William Carlos Williams's
poem about the plums
is not really a poem at all,
but just a note he left on the fridge.
Not to be "smart" or anything,
but I write notes like that all the time
when I drink the last of the OJ or milk.
Mrs. Deyon, are you sure you aren't
reading too much into that poem,
because I don't see how
those critic dudes got that to be
a note to a lover.
I think that's just a hoax to sell poems!
Here's the thing—
I'm a great left fielder
with a .300 batting average.
I can run like Secretariat.
I can solve for x.
But this poetry stuff,
I'm just not getting it!

HOLLY MEYERS

I read an article for art class
about Renaissance man Leonardo da Vinci,
observer, painter, and illustrator.

Meditation and prayer, he claimed,
are ten times more powerful
while sitting in the violet light
shining through a stained-glass window.

Was he not a prototype for creativity?

Why, then, am I sitting in this beige
classroom like every other beige
classroom in the entirely beige

high school trying to write
narrative poetry? I said, "Mr. Callahan,
beige is an originality oxymoron."

He said, "Beige is neutral,
calm, conservative, and relaxing."

None of those words describe me.

That's why I wear something
the color violet to school every day.
I'm purplish-blue.
What color are you?

JASPER TAVERNEY

I was as proud as a peacock
when Mrs. Deyon read my poem to the class.
She wrote *creative* across my verses.
After class, she pulled me aside and told me
she liked my imaginative writing style
and urged me to see someone in guidance
to opt for a more challenging level of instruction.

"Why are you wasting your potential
seeking easy classes?" she asked.
And she added she had noticed
my fine watercolor paintings
hanging outside the art room door.

"Have you considered a career
in the humanities?" she asked.

No one had ever mentioned
my capabilities before. Inspired,
I planned to go to guidance on Monday,
but that night I let Tom talk
me into being a lookout while
he stole a bike from the hardware store.

When I went to his house
on Saturday to tell him I
had not slept all night and
was going to bring the bike back,
he morphed into 'an angry badger.

I never made it to guidance.
I never reached my potential.
Funny thing: one day no one
in the school knows your name.

Next day everyone in the whole
town is reading your life story
splashed across the front page
of the local newspaper.

JUSTICE FAST

Don't
point
your
finger
at
    me
every
time
something
is
missing,
'cause
a lot
of
so-called
good
kids
steal
for
    thrill!
I
only
steal
for
    food!
I'm no
  gangsta,
but I wear a hoodie!

CELINE FONTAINE

Rural Vermont is famous for
Ubiquitous cows and Ben & Jerry,
Neighborly folks and autumn leaves,
Arctic-cold winters in the Northeast Kingdom,
Way too much snow unless you ski,
And Cabot cheese, and maple trees.
Yet, I doubt you've heard of **Runaway Pond**.

Runaway Pond, once known as Long Pond,
Utterly disappeared from sight one
Night because of the not-too-bright
Actions of a team of mill workmen who,
Without thought of consequences,
Attempted to divert the water for their mill.
Young and old alike were shocked and

Ran as fast as they could
Under the fear of death.
North flowed the runaway pond
As quicksand gave
Way and the deluge
Advanced, sweeping away horses, houses,
Yards, barns, fences, cattle, and Long

Pond, the vanishing proof of man's destruction—
One night visible around the bend—
Next day, gone without a trace, so my message:
Doesn't seem smart to mess with nature, eh?

Run away is what I did,
Under the blanket of silent stars.
No one knows why,
And that's how I
Want it to stay.
Attempt to find me, you'll regret
You ever messed with Celine. Got that, eh?

KIM WASHBORNE

Who could believe it?
I thought it was a female problem,
but no! Fifteen years old and diagnosed
with a shark-feeding frenzy
of a stomach cancer.
I sat in the doctor's office and was
told the carnivore inside would
consume my body within the year.

Exhausting treatments,
loss of hair,
doctors offering little hope.
Prognosis—
No prom for me.
No graduation day.
No husband.
No children.
Insides to be devoured by a silent enemy.
Sit and wait to die.

"No! Stop!" I shout.
"No! I won't die!
I'll take the toxic treatment.
I can beat this ravenous foe,"
and so—

I fought to get up every morning.
I fought to endure the medication.
I fought to keep down a quarter of a sandwich.
I fought to stay awake during tutoring.
I fought to endure radiation burns
blistering and searing me inside and out.

Miracle of miracles—my miracle.
I won! I won! I won!
I stood tall
to accept my diploma and
shake hands with Principal Callahan
while the entire class stood and clapped.
Take it from me.
You must fight to defeat
the cancer monster's hunger!
And you can win.

GRAYDON WASHBORNE

So this is how it feels—
like a kick to the groin.
Doubled over in pain,
I realize it was all in vain.
Hope dried up like a crust of bread.
I, the most studious in the class,
read Shakespeare, Steinbeck, and Shaw,
while Marcus read CliffsNotes and comic books,
and copied from any paper he could see.
How did it happen?
I wonder.

I studied the Pythagorean theorem
while Marcus studied the right block.
No one offered me a car.
I, class salutatorian,
got a token scholarship
that won't pay for the books,
and Marcus got a full boat to an Ivy.
I wrote college admissions essays for weeks
while Marcus was courted by college coaches,
even though his highest grade was a C.
How's that fair?

Does it really make sense
that the Super Bowl quarterback makes
more money than the oncologist
who saved Sis's life?

Do we have our priorities right?
Listen to the politicians bicker,
But on a promise, never deliver.

SUKI TAN

I tell my friend, Kim,
"Refuse to die.
Be like the clear jellyfish—
immortal. Regenerate
your missing tummy."

"Overcoming suffering makes you beautiful,"
I tell my friend, Kim.
"Like a kintsugi bowl broken
but mended with gold,
you glitter, my gilded friend.

"Embrace your wounds.
Wounds tell our history.
They don't defeat us."
I tell my friend, Kim,
"Refuse to die!"

ASIA THOMAS

Like Travis Indigo, I write words,
and set them to music.
I record songs for YouTube.
I'm a persistent pop-star wannabe.

Keys, chords, pattern, hook, bridge—
can't forget the chorus.
Listen to my words flow
smooth as maple syrup.

My verses boogie and jive.
Doo-wop! Hip-hop! Or
rap a rhythmic monologue.
Rhyme, or half rhyme?

Decisions.
Keep it all around three minutes.
Advertise.
Move over, Justin Bieber.

I compose lyrics.
I bang beats.
But I don't do blue
since I met you-know-who.

MELODY CAROLL

I am a spunky girl who loves gospel music.
Why can't you sense the beat of my heart? I
hear the rock, rhythm, and blues of America—
see drums, keyboards, and guitars in my dreams.
I want to write blues, ballads, and hip-hop.
I am a soulful girl who loves music.

When I'm singing in a gospel choir,
I feel the presence of a higher being. I
touch the sheet music of the masters,
worrying I'll sing off key like Asia and
cry when I hear the lament of the mourning dove.
I am a spiritual girl who loves music and you.

I understand I must have the faith of a mustard seed.
I say nothing shall be impossible to me. I
dream of singing center stage, hitting high C,
wondering if my sperm-donor Dad's in the audience.
I am a singer who'd swap music to meet my dad.
Wouldn't it be great to live in musical harmony?

FEMI THOMPSON

You lured me in and your hook holds fast.
You snagged me, and I can't yank free.
You snap me like a fly at the end of your line.
Dad was right to want you arrested.

You snagged me, and I can't yank free.
Why did I steal out the window to meet you?
Dad was right to want you arrested.
How you fooled me with your lies.

Why did I steal out the window to meet you?
You cast me aside whenever a new squeeze comes along.
How you fooled me with your lies.
"If you loved me, you would," you said.

You cast me aside whenever a new squeeze comes along.
How many more times will I swallow the bait?
"If you loved me, you would," you said.
You reel me in when you want a night's recreation.

How many more times will I swallow the bait?
You snap me like a fly at the end of your line.
You reel me in when you want a night's recreation.
You lured me in and your hook holds fast.

You're my Miley Cyrus wrecking ball.

You kissed me, Troy, and I melted
like a piece of warm milk chocolate.
Your lips were the first to touch mine,
and I wanted them to linger.

For me, our first kiss was as special
as my dad's hole-in-one,
but you had enjoyed many conquests
and the very next day,
you turned to another, leaving
me with a break-up text,
an aching heart, and a need.

My friends say,
"Can't put a hold on the best
wrestler in the state."

Well, didn't anyone tell you
breaking up is hard to do,
and definitely a text won't suffice?
What's more, it's not nice.

CHLOE HAMPTON

I cry alone
   because my life
      is a crystal champagne flute
         shattered
           by the loss of
              boyfriend
              and
                    best friend in one
                    backstabbing—
                              Betrayal!

KAREN RUSH

"Get away from him while you can."

You warned me when you saw him
bounce me off my locker
like Gram's Raggedy Ann doll.

But I loved him, Mrs. Deyon,
I said, "I think it will get
better once we're married."

You said, "No, it'll only get worse,
and he'll control the purse."

But I did not listen.

Smartest girl in the class,
but a fool for him!

MELANIE ANDREWS

You skipped class—got caught.
Earned an F for plagiarizing.
"Pound your locker."

You have detention for bullying.
You're not in the starting five.
"Pound your locker."

You have math homework.
Your sister gets to drive tonight.
"Pound your locker."

You have to speak to a counselor.
"Pound your locker,
because if you don't,

I'm afraid you'll pound me."
I told Gunther Parker,
"Pound your locker."

Pound your locker,
I said under my breath,
but never to his face.

Dating Gunther Parker:
like walking on hot tarmac
in bare feet.

I got burned.

ACE JACKSON

Blackjack is a game of chance.
Players say, "Hit me," or "Stand."
Melanie begged. "Don't hit me."

TAYLOR PAINE

We read love poems in English class,
by Parker, Shakespeare, Poe, and Browning.
We even read a funny "Valentine" rhyme by Hall.

Mrs. Deyon asked us to write a poem
expressing our feelings about love.
"Will it be realistic, romantic, idealistic,
or humorous?" she asked.

Wearing rose-tinted glasses,
I produced the best love song of my life
and dedicated it to you,
my first love.

I got the first A I'd ever received
for creative writing because I
spilled my heart onto the page.
What a short-lived relationship,
granite-hearted girl.

While I offered eternal love,
you simply sought a prom date.
To you I was a discarded shell
from the bag of peanuts you ate
and crushed on the floor of a roadhouse.

You turned to another, rejected me,
mocked my innocent worship,
and laughed with your friends
at the tender words I
spilled onto the page.

The musician within me tried,
but could not turn the words
into a blues song, 'cause, girl,
you stole the music from my heart.

After I gave in to your begging,
you left me for somebody thinner.
Star basketball players don't want
to be seen with the plumpest cheerleader.
Giggly girls gathered to take my place.
And I got plumper and plumper.

Diet as I did, my rounded body
grew rounder and rounder—
despite the coat I wore to conceal
my secret, which I hid even from myself.
Nurse Lynn asked if I was pregnant,
I said no to her and to myself.
We only did it once!

How I hid the watermelon bulge
from my trusting parents
for eight months remains
a mystery even to me.
When I finally told you, Jordan,
you said …

"I'm too young to be a father.
Weren't you protecting yourself?"

You knew I was too naïve.
Why is the protecting always
the girl's responsibility?
If you knew you were through with me,
why did you beg me to prove my love?
Did you get some perverse pleasure
leaving me alone in such a condition?

JORDAN STANLEY

I know Ashley blames me for her pregnancy,
and her grandmother told the whole town
I carry my mattress on my back,
but there are two sides to every story.
Yes, I told her I loved her once,
but she was the first girl I dated.
Later, when I said I wanted to see other girls,
Ashley cried and clung to me like a tick.
Her vision was for us to be prom royalty,
graduate, go to the same college, and marry.
She and her mother planned my whole life!
I told Ashley it was over.
Then, she suddenly decided we
should act like a married couple
"To cement our relationship."
Like a rat, I fell for the trap
of the bossy girl I'd outgrown.
That night—as most guys would—
I took advantage of her offer,
and for that foolish night,
I mortgaged my life.
Both her parents and mine blame me.
Teachers take her side.
No one seems to understand
I did not know how to break
free from her stranglehold.
I know her pregnancy was a trick
to make me stay, even though she knew
I didn't love her anymore.
I'd told her that numerous times!
Now I work after school and
weekends to save for child support.
And Meredith, my new girlfriend,
is warned about me and treated like a weed
to be uprooted because she sides with me.
Mrs. Deyon, I'm glad you asked us
to write a narrative poem.
It's time someone heard my story!

ACE JACKSON

Rumors spread about Jordan.
Gram doesn't approve of him.
"Wears his mattress on his back."

ACE JACKSON

Arrested—three senior girls.
Criminal charges—jail time.
Spiked teacher's drink—got busted.

JOHNNY NASH

Father,
you buried your troubles in a bottle
until your pickled liver gave out
and our old-fashioned, out-of-touch Mother
brought your ashes home.
We held a vigil in the formal parlor.

After calling hours, Mother put
your urn on the mantle.
Your ever-present shadow
shaded our lives—
six children and a wife
mourning.
Not one of us left whole.

You went to your eternal rest,
but like a moth drawn to light,
I cling to booze.
I live out the legacy
I fear you handed down.

I'd like to think that if you'd known
what would become of us
with your leave-taking,
you'd have tried to delay your departure
by kicking your drinking habit.

However,
since you took your exit stage left
before the first act of my life played out,
I really don't know.

Dad, you're an evanescent memory—
A shooting star on a black night.

I'll never know for sure if
your staying would have
turned out good or bad.

JAMIE SMART

Dad pretends he's perfect.
Watch out for those shifty seagrass eyes.
His sweet-n-sour smile—a dangerous
decoy. Don't be sucked in—
all is not as it seems with him.

By the way, I've heard the whispers
about him and his hottie blonde
intern, but I don't tell because I don't
want to hurt Mom.

Last night Dad got his just rewards.
During his afternoon outburst,
he threw a laundry basket
full of clothes up into the air.

Mom and I rushed around picking
up and putting away our wash before the
minister and his wife arrived for dinner.
In the middle of our meal,

I saw Dad look up at the chandelier in horror.
Mom's eyes followed his gaze.
Forgive me, but I saw my chance
to make him squirm as he had made me

so many times before.
So, I smiled his dishonest smile,
and just as the minister took a bite
of mashed potatoes and gravy,

I said, "Look, Dad, Mom's bra
that you threw earlier is
hanging from the chandelier."
Getting even tastes ambrosial.

Loons laughed on the placid distant lake.
Tails of fireflies
flicked in the tar-black night,
and I was stupid enough to stop
when he pulled his rusted van
along beside me.
How could he do such an atrocity
on such a pure night?

All I wanted was to erase
my school-day concerns.
"Mom, let me walk to the store
for the loaf of bread.
No need to take the car."
Such a simple request
after a hectic exam day.

For the sensation-driven media,
I'm a story.
But I'm somebody's daughter.
The pervert makes me
watch TV every night to hear *his* story.

Newscasters say rumors fly at school.
I listen as my poor sister tries
to defend me from the slanders.
No! I did not run away with some boy.
No! I did not have a blowup
fight with my mom.

I cannot bear another night
of this maniacal monster's foul breath!

JENNY VARIN
AN EPISTLE TO MY SISTER

Emily, expectation for the day
You would be returned loomed over us
like an anticipated tax refund check.

Dad lost his job because his energy was sucked
from his body by the giant vacuum cleaner
that was the disappearance of You,
his eldest daughter.

Mother blamed herself for letting You go alone.
I defended You from the speculation and lies,
but truthfully, Emily, I sometimes blamed You.

I was a ruined sweater
mistakenly thrown into the dryer.
I never could be
the daughter our parents mourned,
or the perky cheerleader the coach adored.

It is not easy to grow up in a house of pain,
or in a school where whispers
tell the new student, "Jenny had a sister.
She vanished on a dark night."

We thought all we wanted was to know
who took You, and where You went.
Trapped four years in a purgatory
of endless, empty, unrewarding clues,
we sought answers about Your whereabouts—
then—*the call* from the sheriff came.

As part of a plea bargain, a wife
caught robbing a bank with her husband
turned against him to reduce her sentence.

She told of how her husband grabbed You,
how he hid and tortured You, and later,
because she had become jealous
and threatened to reveal his secret,
how he finally killed You.

53

Buried Your battered body nearby,
in an abandoned silo adjacent to our cornfield,
and all the time the police followed clues
of sightings from shore to distant shore,
your abductor had stored Your body like silage
under our noses, mocking our Adirondack town, and
planning to rob the bank as he had robbed us of You.

ACE JACKSON

Who set the deck against us?
Dealer shuffled; someone cut.
What busted us was pure trust.

TROY RUSH

Known for my wiry body
and happy-go-lucky attitude,
I'm a well-strung guitar,
proud to be the best
wrestler in the county.
My pranks entertain my classmates,
making school life interesting.
I don't worry if I end up spending
a period or two in detention.
These are my glory days,
but before I graduate and go off
to join the US Marines,
I have a few parting questions.

Mrs. Deyon,
remember when I told you
I smelled alcohol on Coach Decker's breath?
Remember when I said he had a bottle in his desk?
You said, "Oh, I don't think so, dear."
Do you believe me now that he's been arrested,
found passed out drunk in the driver's seat,
with his car door hanging open for all to see?

What do you think,
now that his wife drives him
to work every day
because he's lost his license?

Now he knows how I felt,
benched for breaking rules.
Quite the example, wouldn't you say?
Is that a little of that
irony you talked about, Mrs. Deyon?

Just an innocent little question or two
to let you know
I've been thinking things over.
Ha-ha.

CHARLOTTE EMO

Hangin' with my peeps,
I wanna scream and shout,
and let it out!
You never escape high school.

I'm one of the senior proud,
I'm the cement of the clique.
We mark, identify, and label.
We pigeonhole, exclude, and judge.

Nerd, loner, jock?
We don't let you in.
"Conceal, don't feel."
That's our mantra!

At Mountain Valley High, souls are bare.
Rumors spread like the flu.
Everybody knows your name.
Everybody knows your game.

We're sleek thoroughbreds,
racing toward the finish line.
Scream and shout and let us out!

MARCUS COOPER

Not so fast, girls;
me and my bros manipulate.
We're the jocks, masterminds, and wingmen.
We turn you into putty
and your names we muddy.
You're putty, putty, putty
in our gritty hands.
We throw you like clay.
We caress and shape you.
Mary, Lydia, Ashley, Chloe.
We fire you up.
We mold you into statues.
You're twisted figures
we love till we hate.
Then, we turn to the next fresh,
green lump of clay,
"Hup, hup, march on—
till we reach the end game."

REESE WONDERALL

Charlotte, Monica, and I wanted
a Friday the thirteenth diversion.
Since Grandma's house overlooks
Yelling Cemetery and the moon was full,
the setting primed our mood.

We saw the TV report
of a prison escape.
Halloween loomed.
I grabbed the Ouija board
from my grandma's closet.

Ouija, "Who will Charlotte marry?"
"Will Monica get a date to the dance?"
"Will Reese find true love?"

We followed with taboo questions,

and we waited for the answers,
which were none of our business …
a shadow drifted across the mirror.

We looked up and, honest to God,
there was a rope swinging.
"Why is that rope hanging outside the window?"

Screaming and crying, we ran,
abandoning the room
and Ouija.

I cannot tell you the rest.
The three of us made a solemn pact
never to reveal the truth
of what happened on that terrifying
night on Graveyard Lane
at the Yelling Cemetery.

HANK HUGHES

Reese and her friends made a pact,
but I didn't. Still, I can't reveal
what happened on that terrifying night
on Graveyard Lane. *Sorry, Mama.*

Mama, you warned me to be careful.
Said, "I'd rather you stay home.
It's Friday the thirteenth,
and my blood's curdling like month-old milk."

"Mama, we need the money. I'm
gonna finish raking Mrs. Jacob's
leaves, and come right home."
Those were the last words we
ever exchanged. *Sorry, Mama.*

After finishing my work, I
decided to take a shortcut home
through the Yelling Cemetery.
Sorry, Mama.
Just as I reached the gate,
the three girls screamed and ran.

As I stood like a deer in headlights,
watching them flee the mausoleum,
the sheriff's cruiser arrived on the scene.
Sirens blared. *Sorry, Mama*
Pop! Pop! Ka-pow!

Sorry, Mama!
Oh, sooo sorry.

ACE JACKSON

Sheriff thought he saw a gun,
but there was none in Hank's hand
Poor black kid drew the wrong card.

59

YOLANDA CASTINE

No one just like me
in my vanilla homeroom.
Even my mother has a pale
face, like the fresh cream
I beat in our stainless-steel bowl.
How could this be, I ask?

My bigoted, grouchy Grandmother
glares at my mother.
Mother retreats like a hermit crab
into her shell, but no one will give me
the answer. I remain an enigma,
even to myself—one peerless soul—
a Mona Lisa.

In Home and Careers class, I
select a pattern.
Somehow, I think I can ease
the pain, sewing
twenty black-and-white fabric
remnants into a zebra motif.

"May we play music while we sew?"
a classmate asks.
I listen to Lady Gaga's lyrics in
"Born This Way," and suddenly,
it's all good—
I'm okay in my skin.

When I get older,
I'll find my dad.
Woo-hoo!

LILY KELLY

Nightly, I sleep in a cozy bed in a farmhouse
a short stride from our country's northern border.
Rumor says my home has a proud history.
In response to the Fugitive Slave Act,
did this house come to be a safety net?
Are there secrets dark as molasses
it will not divulge?
Did runaways sleep under our gray slate roof?
Was one slave saved
from the master's cruel whip?
Was my great-grandmother a conductor
on the road to Canada and freedom?
Did Great-Gram hang a code on our clothesline?
According to legend, a black center
square on a log cabin quilt symbolized a
safe haven for runaways before
and during the Civil War.
My frayed quilt has such a pattern.
Many times, I heard Grandma say this quilt
must be passed down
to the oldest daughter
because it's a family heirloom
reflecting our proud history.
If she were alive now, I'd ask her,
"Was this worn quilt I sleep under
used as a signal of a welcoming shelter?"
I would like to think so.

DEIRKS LANDLEY

Horse, smack, skag,
Every day abuse. Each
Rush screamed for more
Opiate—Emma's obsession.
I had to free my sister from her
Need. She went to any length to score her stash.

Heroin was her forbidden lover.
Emma was hooked on her abusive paramour.
Really panicked me. She
Opened and snorted a powder-filled button.
In a greedy hunger hidden from my parents, she
Needed and went to any length to get high.

GOING
DOWN
DOWN
DOWN

CRASH!
BANG!
BOOM!

Help! Help! I called a hotline to yank
Emma from heroin's clutches after she hit
Rock bottom—overdosed and shattered like a crystal doll.
Outgoing, charismatic, and loyal sister turned
Into a desperate junkie, compelling my big-brother intervention.
Now life's normal—Emma's shed her sleazy ex.

CASEY ARO

Chopped a line,
inhaled pure-white Molly.
Molly and I mingled
time after time,
not so pure—
white, beige, brown—
frenemy.
High from a hit of molecular
ecstasy.
Molly and I
night crawlers
loving everyone
dancing
to the bass-driven music
ecstasy
drifting
down
No prying brother like Emma to intervene
Down
      Down
         Drifting
            Down
               Down
                  Crack!

ACE JACKSON

Ambulance called to the school.
Casey overdosed at ten.
I loved her, but she loved crack.

KENDRA WILSON

Teacher said write about what you know.
Well, here is what I know:
Those protestors
who picket outside abortion clinics
were nowhere to be found when I
was being fed stale, moldy green bread
while my foster mother's "real" daughters
ate fresh homemade bread and meat for lunch.

I wondered if it would have been
better not to have been born than to be me—
treated like a smelly sneaker,
and fed the bruised fruit while
the "real family" ate the pick of the crop.

Do you have any idea what it did
to my self-esteem to be treated
like a leper in my so-called home?

Why didn't the social services workers
ask why the refrigerator door wore a padlock,
keeping me from getting a snack?

When the guidance counselor
eventually helped my brother and me find
our real mom, that was no better.
She came and took us away, but
alcohol was her real baby.
I was left to fend for myself,
and my brother, Jim, forced to join the service
with two wars being waged.

Paige can't write wrongs. But
lawmakers, you could. What do you know
about life for the unwanted child?
Better yet, what have you tried to learn?

Looks to me like you forgot
babies become unwanted children.
That sums up what I know.

SHANNON TRAYNOR

Dear Mom, I'm the daughter you chose to abandon.
Deep in my gut and bones I knew you were out there.
But another man and woman gave me their name.

Dear Mom, was I conceived during uncontrolled passion?
I found you, but phantom father's identity you refuse to share.
But another man and woman gave me their name.

Dear Mom, did you take time to meet your stand-in?
Deep in my soul when she beat me, I prayed you'd care.
But another man and woman gave me their name.

Dear Mom, do you know you dumped me with a cold witch?
She never rocked me in a chair or gave me a teddy bear.
But another man and woman gave me their name.

Dear Mom, adoptive parents branded me *Shannon*.
So unfair, not an ounce of love for me could they spare.
But another man and woman gave me my name.

Dear Mom, did you think I'd want to live in a mansion?
I swear, I craved your kiss on my cheek more than air.
But another man and woman gave me my name.

Out of your womb, wrinkled and wonky, I came.
But another man and woman gave me my name.
Why didn't you keep me and give me your name,
 Dear Mom?

MATTHEW RAM

When someone spiked the punch
at the senior banquet, I came
home to you, Mother,
and confessed I have no
desire for girls.

You cried and screamed,
"I don't know what
we could have done
for God to have given
us—"

I won't say the word

"—as a child."

Since you're a proud believer,
I was hoping for a hug.
It's plain to see you want
to sweep me into the cellar.

Say no more.
I'll grab my bags,
and head out the door.

Pray for us both, Mother.

ACE JACKSON

No-count gambler, that's my dad.
Luck ran out in the back room
and so did my queen mother

ACE JACKSON

Dad doubled down on eleven.
Dealer beat him with a seven.
He should have come home sooner.

The dealer shuffles. We cut.
Life's a gambling game some lose.
But the question, "Who will win?"

JANE DOVE

With a murder of crows cawing nearby,
he goes, "If I was to shoot you right now,
where would you want to be shot—
in your head, in your back, or in your chest?"

And then I hear him messing with the gun.
And he counts to three,
and pulls the trigger.

And I am still alive.

When I open my eyes,
I just see him laughing.
After he and others break me,
doing horrifying acts I can't talk about,

he asks me if I am hungry.
I tell him no,
but he puts a dog biscuit in my mouth.
And he shoves me into a dog crate.

Abuse after abuse for forty days—
captive, beaten, and worse.
Beware of the internet, the tool
he used to catch and sell my roommate,

his other hostage. She tricks
him—how, I do not know—
and escapes. When the police
come, he jumps out the window,

leaving me crushed into a drawer
under the bed. I hear someone
calling my name, but am too
frightened to answer. I lie

stiff as a stake and shaking.
And Officer Pearly pulls
the drawer open and says,
"Oh my God!"

I hug him, and my knees give out.
A predator owned me, but
Now I'm free.
Paige, thanks for reporting me as missing.

No thanks to you, Montel.
I saw you hiding in the shadows
when Payne grabbed me.
Why didn't you help?

I escaped my nightmare, but hear gossip.
Sorry about Emily, Emma, and Hank.
Charlotte may be right:
"You never escape high school,
but there are worse places to be."

AISHA KOFI

On September 11, 2001,
I was less than a year old,
living with my parents in a brownstone
in our state's capital,
nowhere near New York City;
but because my father makes me
live under the veil,
I am as unwelcome
in this school as a fly
at the dinner table.
My classmates see nothing
but the hijab.
Need I say more?

YBETH HERMANA

No need to give me advice.
You do not have to tell me
I should not rush to start
dating handsome boys.

You do not have to warn me.
I have heard the words,
sweet as coconut milk.

When my sisters were courted,
I hid under the frayed sofa
and learned the promises to resist.
Jesus assured Bianca she
would possess riches galore.
If diapers to wash make you rich,
she's the wealthiest twenty-year-old
in the whole row of squalid shacks.

Fueled by passion and desire,
Jorge vowed eternal love and devotion.
Tears well in my eyes as I see
Alita holding two toddlers' hands
and toting a baby in her swollen belly
while she shops for dinner.

I've seen my delicate, gentle sisters
turn into tired, worn-out victims,
hopelessly existing in a prison
created by love and unfounded trust.

I'll rely on college and career
to break the cycle from the life I see.

Braceros, do not come to woo me!
"Tienen que tener cuidado!"

You have to be careful,
I tell my younger sisters.

MIRANDA AQUI

To you, I'm a skulking silhouette, avoiding the open corridor.
When I see Customs patrolling, I make the sign of the cross.
We stole across the border, hiding under night's moonlit quilt.

The coyote aided us and charged us a fortune, though we're poor.
We fear detection, but borrowed money binds Dad to a foreign boss.
To you, I'm a skulking silhouette, avoiding the open corridor.

We're wolves lurking, learning life's lessons outside the school door.
Haters treat us like garbage they'd like to toss.
We stole across the border, hiding under night's moonlit quilt.

I followed my parents, but fear of discovery chills me to the core.
We didn't stand in line, so debt hangs from Dad's neck like an albatross.
To you, I'm a skulking silhouette, avoiding the open corridor.

In one school I meet Ross, a quarterback, I adore.
Because of my paranoia, I don't flirt with Ross.
We stole across the border, hiding under night's moonlit quilt.

I dwell in tenant farmers' shacks I abhor.
I'm the cinnamon-skinned prey immigration agents seek to oust.
To you, I'm a skulking silhouette, avoiding the open corridor.
With a family of *hermanos* just like me, I hide under a guilt quilt.

ANNA LABOWSKI

After a long passage over rough seas,
my ancestors entered this country
through Ellis Island, legally, but
no less hungry or desperate than
Miranda's family of illegal workers.

Into the bowels of the iron mines
my ancestors tread, to owe their souls
to the company store. "Does their
plight sound familiar?" I ask Miranda.

Into the mills the child laborers plodded.
Returned home after ten-hour shifts,
fighting the ice-cold wind and the snow
swirling around their poorly-clad bodies.

Labor unions fought to save the appendages
of children like my great-grandfather—
sent to unclog the hungry machines
that chewed the arms of unsuspecting boys—
who served as sweatshop sacrifices
to appease the manmade industry gods.

After stealing their way across the border,
children like Miranda's brothers get up early,
and pile into the bed of a dilapidated pickup truck.
Avoiding the truant officer, into the fields they tread,
skipping school to pick crops from sunup to sundown.

The lady in the harbor says, "Give me your tired,
your poor ..."

I ask, "Why?"

My boyfriend, Terry Billings, says,
"Ka-ching! Ka-ching! Ka-ching!"

TOBY TINKER

"Cry, tubby Toby," they taunt,
and I obey.
I eat so much, I waddle—
I'm the bullies' prey.
Persecutors call me hippo,
but how can I push away
from my cafeteria tray?

I listen as Dad accuses Mom.
She can't go to the store
without taking one of us!
He's insecure, grass-green jealous—
fears she'll run off with the first
salesman who gives her attention.

Six kids in the family, but
I'm the one who can't forget the fists,
Mom's black eyes—the sobbing, or
worse yet, Dad's day-after apologies.

So I surrender
to a piece of chocolate cake
with a pint-size side of ice cream.

ACE JACKSON

It's a gamble when you press.
One too many and you lose.
Ever heard, "His luck ran out?"

ACE JACKSON

Ross and Troy better cool it.
Noel's a time bomb. Tick-tock.
I'm going to cash in my chips.

CORA SIMMONS

Wait-listed.
Standing on the sideline again,
praying to be admitted.

Through no fault of my own,
trying to squeeze into any spot
away from Mountain Valley High.

Ranked third in the class,
but Dad didn't sign the financial
aid forms on time. I go to the

mailbox, praying. *Please, God,*
let me escape our Airstream home
with its barbed-wire fence. And

it's there—my ticket out of here.
"I am pleased to congratulate you
on your acceptance into ..."

ACCEPTED!
ACCEPTED!
ACCEPTED—finally, I'm accepted.

I don't care if a blizzard
blows through town tomorrow.
I'm accepted into college.
Let the Regents begin.

I don't care about dumb volleyball.
Sitting on the sideline's not a problem.
I'm almost out of here.
I'm accepted into the University of Florida.

Let the sun shine on me.

HUNTER NORTH

Why did I love a girl who didn't love me?
Someone should have warned me.
You can't control the one you fall for.
Is it hormones driving me wild?

Stormi swept me up in her windstorm.
Twisted my heart like a tin roof in a tornado.
Without warning, spit my love at my feet.
Someone should have warned me.

Stalkers lurking in shadows don't offer love.
Someone should have cautioned Jane Dove.
From deep inside, I'm drawn to Jane.
Would it be insensitive to tell her?

I want to take a chance on love once more.
Is Jane the girl who could love me?
Will she fall for me, or does she want more?
If I approach her, will she flee?

Is it too soon to ask her for a date?

What is my destiny?
Could someone please tell me?
Will I help Jane forget the click of the gun?
Or when I speak, will she run?

Life's better when two become one.

RUBY O'BRIEN

My hoverboard caught on fire.
That's why my homework is late.
Couldn't write—smoke in my eyes.
Don't blame me for what was fate.

ZOEY JUBERT

We're dressed in short, grass-green skirts,
on a crisp, fall day. Snow spits in the air,
but I'm hotter than a woodstove in January.
My heart thumps a feverish, hungry beat.

We want—need—this win. Last chance
to taste its silky, sweet, smooth-as-fudge
flavor. My teammates fire off three shots
in three minutes. Our penalty corner fails.

Running. Passing. All hopes on a big win.
We're in a frenzy—frantic.
The score stuck—tied at three.
Sudden-death overtime—now or never.

Seconds left on the clock. Marisol
passes the spherical-hard-plastic-
dimpled ball to me. My pulse quickens—
heart beats in staccato-lightning flashes.

Sweaty hands grip bowed sticks.
I position the ball on the grass.
With stick upright, knees bent—on automatic—
I stare into the keeper's eyes,

take a small backswing,
shift weight from back to front foot,
turn, fake, slap toward the corner,
and follow through. Breathe…

The crowd roars. Score!
I'm a hero for the moment.
We're state field hockey champs.
Trophy gives our team immortality.

NOEL TRIP

Like buzzards over roadkill,
you circle me in the locker room.
Do you really think it lifts you up
to inflict pain on me and take me down?

You gang up on me to amuse yourselves,
and because you're the jocks, the popular guys,
Coach laughs and says it's only in fun.
Fun for whom? The faculty
nurtures you and your buddies.

Well, I am not Toby.
I don't eat grief bacon. But
next week the psychs will
analyze the *whys* and the *hows*.

Any science student could give them a hint.
Look no further than the bullies you've fed.
Add vinegar to baking soda
and what do you get?

Chemists, not shrinks
will be needed to probe
the next not-so-spontaneous
school explosion.

Watch out, Ross,
it's your last lunch
at Mountain Valley High.
Tonight, like me,
you'll miss the Senior Ball.

Boom!

ACE JACKSON

Tragedies still shock and thrill
when they happen on school grounds.
Toby cried and Noel shot.

Fifty-two of us face down.
Lady Luck ran out on Ross.
Noel exploded at lunch.

TRAVIS INDIGO
ELEGY FOR NOEL TRIP

Ain't it a shame, words—
jagged and cutting like barbed wire—
drove Noel to unleash his ire.
Thoughts as deep, dark, and cold
as an Adirondack lake made him bold.

Ain't it a shame school life
is a blues song full of strife?
For the odd one out we gave no time.
One abreast he trod, with no rhythm or rhyme.

From whom did we learn to hate?
Why did we take the bait?
Why do parents and friends of our ilk
train us to mimic no flies in the milk?

Ain't it a shame Mrs. Deyon won't
forget his name. Brilliant,
remote loner dressed in black.
Aimed at beating hearts and didn't hold back.
Don't hold back.

We choked on sobs as we sang all night long.
Bipolar or not, what he did was dead wrong.
You can ask, was he sick or an evil spawn?
Without a gun, could he have drawn?

Screams echoed in theaters and shopping malls.
Gunshots reverberated through school halls.
Vulnerable, tragic, perfect victims that they took.
Noel will join them in the history book.

Ain't it a shame Mrs. Deyon
won't forget his name. Brilliant,
remote loner dressed in black.
Aimed at beating hearts and didn't hold back.
Life's a blues song in a backpack.

KELLY FINLEY

Just sayin'…
We're packin' up,
ready to end this school year.
Classes ended.
Regents passed.

We've shed weighty backpacks,
and Mrs. Deyon's gonna retire,
but I gotta comment here,
before we exit with hearts
heavy as body-building barbells.

Life's a blues song for some.
But for my brother and me,
life's a good part celebration.

We danced and shared words
in the halls of this old school.
We played ball in the afternoons,
if there wasn't any hayin' to do.

Mama taught us to smile
and to make our love true.
And that's what we're gonna do.
Let the school bell ring!

We plan to spread lyrics and music.
Gospel, country, and bluegrass—
we'll pick strings wherever we go.
Add a bit o' banter, you've got our cure for sad.

We sing as we rise.
Rise like the phoenix!
Don't stop the music!
Join the party cries.

We won't let dreams die.
We're on an Adirondack high.
Tonight, we graduate, and say good-byes.
We promise we won't forget our ties.

ACE JACKSON

I should have said our good-byes,
it wasn't in my cards.
Evan Last gets what he wants.

MRS. DEYON

Parents, you shaped.
The clay molded on your potter's wheels—
my students.

When students carried
their Blues to me, like a sculptor,
I cut through protective layers
opaque as onion skins.

Students didn't write subtle.
Sincere words and insights
flowed in hormone-driven rhythms.

Embellished lyrics exposed
snippets of private lives.
In the halls, gossip hummed
unguarded truths.

Because I listened,
my reluctant poets revealed
secrets scratched on lined paper.

Experiences not bared to busy mothers
bled from cracked vessels onto pages
shared with me, spilling
perspectives singular as snowflakes.

One must handle teens carefully.
Like fragile pottery,
they are formed, ready to be
fired, but not yet hardened.

EVAN LAST

Mrs. Deyon tried to keep me here
for another year. Well,
it ain't gonna happen.
I tried to read what
she threw at us
like a curve ball … but
asking me to write a poem
was really down
and in my face.

Here's how the semester played out:

Whitman sang for himself.
"Bean Eater" Gwendolyn Brooks
got real cool.
The raven quoted, "Nevermore."
Thoreau built a house for twenty-eight dollars,
twelve-and-one-half cents, and traveled
to the beat of a different drummer.
Richard Cory went home
and put a bullet through his head.
Noel snapped.

I broke down and wrote a poem
for English class
so I could graduate—
and Emily Dickinson's head popped off!

PART II

IGNITE

THE FIRE WITHIN

IGNITE THE FIRE WITHIN

Ever wanted to compose a poem or the lyrics to a song? Is an assignment to write a poem for English class hanging over your head like a storm cloud? Or do you want to win an upcoming poetry slam (a competition in which poets recite original poetry)? This book was written for you. I'm optimistic it will help give voice to the poet within you. Please feel free to use it as a tool to improve your craft. I hope it inspires you to share the poems you write with confidence.

By reading and writing poetry, we understand others better. We're more likely to survive, and perhaps even to live in harmony. Feelings are important. People matter. Robert Frost understood that. He once said, "I am not a nature poet. There is almost always a person in my poems." Read his poem titled "Birches," and decide what he is saying about nature, youth, love, and death. Whether you believe he was a pessimist, optimist, or realist, I hope you'll see that his work hides a subtlety. Subtlety makes for powerful poetry.

Siri, the virtual assistant Noah refers to in the poem "Noah Newman," cannot write poetry yet. Although the question-answering computer system Watson beat Ken Jennings, game show contestant extraordinaire, on *Jeopardy*, no artificial intelligence has been programmed to write good poetry. Bots lack a sense of compassion, emotional depth, and freshness in the use of language.

Don't many websites make us prove we aren't robots? Only people possess passion and common sense. Free from emotional, physical, and mental baggage, robots can be faster than humans, but they cannot see things from another person's perspective. Poets can.

Writing poetry isn't about winning a race or answering questions faster than the next guy or gal. It's about using language and craft in such a manner as to share meaning, giving the listener or reader more than an answer to a question.

What is poetry? Carl Sandburg, the American author famous for the "Fog" poem I refer to in this anthology, said, "Poetry is an echo, asking a shadow to dance." German writer and statesman Johann Wolfgang von Goethe, said, "Personality is everything in art and poetry." What did they mean? To me, poetry possesses a quality only humans can capture.

Before writing good poetry, we must read poetry. Sometimes we may choose to mirror the poetry we enjoy. Other times, we may decide to cut a new path. Whether we travel to the beat of Thoreau's "different drummer," ignoring the rules of formatting and punctuation which poets before us followed, or stick to traditions, we should continue to read poetry. Goals to consider: Read both classic and contemporary poetry every day, and write daily.

I hated poetry until an English teacher introduced E. E. Cummings's poetry to my classmates and me. After reading "anyone lived in a pretty how town," I clung to the poem like a base stealer clinging to second base. I loved that Cummings broke rules. The only word he capitalized in the poem was *Women* (how intriguing). Why? What was his relationship with women? Questions materialized. Once he sparked my budding feminist and poetic interests, I read and enjoyed a variety of poems.

What makes good poetry? To be characterized as good, poems must be clear to the intended audience. When I became a high school English teacher, I wanted my students to read and enjoy poetry. To share my love for poetry, I introduced poetry they could identify with, or at least understand.

If you began reading *Backpack Blues* with the attitude, *I don't get poetry*, I hope you are rethinking. The lyrics of songs are often poems put to music. Before reading and discussing Edwin Arlington Robinson's "Richard Cory," listen to the song version from Simon & Garfunkel's *Sounds of Silence* album. Find and read the lyrics to Queen's "The Show Must Go On" before listening to the song. Isn't that poetry?

Poems like Robert Hayden's "The Whipping" rang true with many of my students. Unfortunately, too many could identify. The poem provides an excellent way to lead into a discussion of point of view and abuse. While teachers urge students to stick to one point of view when writing, this poem demonstrates how breaking the sticking-to-one-point-of-view rule can help the poet present theme. Have you read the poem? If not, I suggest you do. Follow this link: https://allpoetry.com/The-Whipping

"The Whipping" demonstrates the concept of empathy (fellow feeling) which we adopt after a senseless tragedy, an Olympic victory, falling in love, or when we view another person being bullied.

Once you enjoy reading poetry, you'll be ready to write your own poems. So I recommend you continue reading and find a place to practice writing. Get the words out of your head and onto the paper or computer screen. Revise later.

According to an article I once read, Agatha Christie wrote while sitting in the bathtub, chomping on apples. I don't write that way, but inspiration may come at any time and any place. To be safe, write when inspiration happens. If the words are trying to claw their way out of your brain, write them down before you forget them.

In *On Writing*, Stephen King recommends having a quiet place to go to write. Elizabeth Sims, author of *You've Got a Book in You*, says a writer should have a garret (an attic or loft). E. B. White, author of *Charlotte's Web* and *Stuart Little*, sought refuge in a cabin to compose his works. He also liked to sit at a simple white desk, watching farm animals or even a gray spider on the wall. Truman Capote found his place to write in hotel rooms. Florida novelist Tim Dorsey gets inspiration from seedy motels. If I ever get rich, my haven will be someplace where I can see sparkling blue water or a babbling mountain brook, not a seedy hotel. Give me a serene setting and watch my fingers tap the keyboard. Find your writing spot.

What time of day are you most productive? These days, I write best when I get up early. When I was younger, I wrote at night. Your writing time might change over the years. Most of the writers I know or have read about like to write before other members of their households awake, but one friend prefers to write after the other members of his family retire for the night. The choice is the writer's, but try to be consistent.

Want to be a writer? I recommend you find your hideaway. Get a journal or notepad. Have sticky notes and blank white envelopes (scrap paper) available so you can jot down thoughts before they disappear like home runs over a fence or bubbles in your bubble bath. Never leave home without a pen and notebook at your disposal, or, for those connected to devices, a cell phone with a notepad. That may work for you. I know a slam poet who writes poems and saves them on his smartphone. For me, the keyboard helps. Most of my friends prefer a pen or pencil.

Experience on both sides of the teacher's desk taught me that teens enjoy reading about other teens with whom they can empathize, sympathize, and identify. Do you? To make the world a little less lonely, to include the alienated, to reach reluctant poets, to provide patterns for composing poems, I wrote *Backpack Blues*, a Royal Palm Literary Award First-Place winner, inspired by Edgar Lee Masters's *Spoon River Anthology*.

I challenge you to go to your haven to write your own poems. The following pages will guide you through the process if you need help. Hopefully, the poems in *Backback Blues* have inspired you to step up to the computer and write.

Questions? Go to my website.

http://www.melodydeandimick.com

Click *Contact Melody*. I'll try to answer your questions in a timely fashion.

Gadgets in the Poetic Equipment Bag

Athletes cannot play sports without equipment. Carpenters need tools. Poets also need a few utensils in order to write. A pitcher doesn't use the same pitch for every batter. If he did, batters would know what to expect. Soon they would be hitting off him every time they stepped into the batter's box. Poets need the same element of surprise that pitchers need.

Likewise, a cabinetmaker doesn't use every tool in the box to make a drawer, but without a variety of tools, the cabinets might not hang properly. Let's examine the tools and techniques poets use.

Alliteration

Alliteration is defined as the repetition of the initial consonant sounds of words in a succession.

Example from "Shannon Traynor" in *Backpack Blues*:

> *Out of your womb, wrinkled and wonky, I came.*

The consonant *w* is repeated.

Example from "Deirks Landley":

> ***Help! Help!** I called a **h**otline to yank / Emma from **h**eroin's clutches after she **h**it.*

Which consonant is repeated?

Allusion

Writers often allude (refer) to persons or things in the Bible, mythology, history, or literature. The allusion should be used to make the poem clearer—more visual. While good writers make use of allusions, they use them sparingly so as not to appear to be pedantic (showing off knowledge like Sheldon on the sitcom, *The Big Bang Theory*). Attempt to use allusions most people won't have to look up in order to understand your poem. As salt adds flavor to our french fries, allusions add flavor to our poetry.

Examples from *Backpack Blues*:

> *We didn't stand in line, so debt hangs from Dad's neck like an albatross.*

This refers, (alludes) to the poem, *The Rime of the Ancient Mariner*, by Samuel Taylor Coleridge. After reading *The Rime of the Ancient Mariner*, you can understand the allusion. Having a dead albatross hanging from your neck is not a good thing.

> *On September 11, 2001 / I was less than a year old / living with my parents in a brownstone / in our state's capital / nowhere near New York City.*

The allusion (reference) is to the infamous terrorist attack on the Twin Towers in New York City.

What does Peggy McIntosh's knapsack allude to in the first "Paige Hacker" poem? If you don't know who she was, Google this link: https://www.newyorker.com/books/page-turner/the-origins-of-privilege. How does knowing who she was add to the meaning of the poem?

"Evan Last" contains six allusions to literature and one allusion to the sport of baseball. Can you locate them? How do they add to the humor of the poem?

If you've ever played or watched a game of baseball, what do you know about a pitch that is down and low?

What is Evan saying he thinks about Mrs. Deyon's poetry-writing assignment?

The final line of the collection says, "Emily Dickinson's head popped off!"

Why? How does that line relate to a definition of poetry Emily Dickinson once made? Should "Evan Last" end the collection?

Assonance

Sometimes poets repeat vowel sounds in words close to each other, creating assonance. The repetition of vowel sounds in poetry is called *assonance*.

From "Elegy for Noel Trip, Written by Travis Indigo":

Why do parents and friends of our ilk / train us to mimic no flies in the milk?

The vowel *i* is repeated.

Brevity

Keep poems brief. Every word must show. Compress. Cull the superfluous embellishments. Unless you are writing a ballad, consider keeping the poem to one or two pages.

Many people enjoy the haiku, a traditional form of Japanese poetry consisting of three lines. The first and last lines of a haiku have five syllables; the middle line has seven syllables. The lines of the seventeen-syllable haiku rarely rhyme. Though the haiku form takes brevity to a minimalist level, some refer to Shel Silverstein's couplet from "Fleas" as the world's shortest poem: "Adam / Had 'em."

I tend to be a little wordier. My mentor, Peggy Miller, introduced me to the blackjack poem, a twenty-one-syllable poem. The blackjack poem consists of three lines of seven syllables each. Every one-stanza "Ace Jackson" poem in this anthology is a blackjack poem. Sometimes I chose to write Ace Jackson poems of more than one stanza. In those cases, each stanza contains twenty-one syllables.

ACE JACKSON

You call me the knave of hearts.
But listen to my gossip.
Foul rumors spread like tumors.

It was my intention to use the Ace Jackson poems as the cement to join the poems into an anthology of a singular Mountain Valley High School senior class. Did it work for you? What would your anthology look like if you wrote about your class? Which classmates would stand out as: Bullies? Victims? Heroes? Artistic? Troubled? Popular? Cool?

Couplets

Couplets, lines that usually rhyme and have the same meter, are often the building blocks of rhyming poetry. Rhyming calls notice to the word, making it the focal point, or center of attention, of the line. It caps off the line before it.

In general, poets seek a strong word to end a line. Writer Mary Burton, the modern queen of the suspense novel, told the audience at a conference I attended that she attempts to end the sentences in her novels with a strong verb. Although I don't write much rhyming poetry, I often try to include a surprise twist by ending my poems with a couplet.

Examine the witches' language in Shakespeare's *Macbeth* from poemhunter.com. How many couplets can you find? Are the last words of the couplets strong words?

Song of the Witches: "Double, double toil and trouble"
By William Shakespeare

Double, double toil and trouble;
Fire burn and caldron bubble.
Fillet of a fenny snake,
In the caldron boil and bake;
Eye of newt and toe of frog,
Wool of bat and tongue of dog,
Adder's fork and blind-worm's sting,
Lizard's leg and owlet's wing.
For a charm of powerful trouble,
Like a hell-broth boil and bubble.

...
Double, double toil and trouble;
Fire burn and caldron bubble.

Cool it with a baboon's blood,
Then the charm is firm and good.

One of my favorite Shakespearean couplets appears at the end of his "Sonnet 130," which is often referred to as the "Dark Lady" sonnet. How does the couplet turn the poem from a seeming insult of his lover to a compliment?

Sonnet 130

My mistress' eyes are nothing like the sun;
Coral is far more red than her lips' red;
If snow be white, why then her breasts are dun;
If hairs be wires, black wires grow on her head.
I have seen roses damasked, red and white,
But no such roses see I in her cheeks;
And in some perfumes is there more delight
Than in the breath that from my mistress reeks.
I love to hear her speak, yet well I know
That music hath a far more pleasing sound;
I grant I never saw a goddess go;
My mistress when she walks treads on the
    ground.
And yet, by heaven, I think my love as rare
As any she belied with false compare.

Enjambment

According to the online *Oxford Dictionary, enjambment* in verse "is the continuation of a sentence without a pause beyond the end of a line, couplet, or stanza." Some people write one-sentence poems without one punctuation mark. The role of enjambment is to let an idea carry on beyond the restrictions of a single or, even, multiple lines.

I use enjambment in "Chloe Hampton." I don't want the reader to pause until the dash. My purpose is to stress the word *Betrayal*. What else did I do to stress *Betrayal*?

Google and read "The Red Wheelbarrow" by William Carlos Williams to see how Williams uses enjambment.

Note how enjambment gives a poem a fast pace.

End-Stopped Line

Simply put, an end-stopped line is a line of poetry with a punctuation mark at the end. The punctuation mark indicates a pause.

Foot

Each unit of rhythm in poetry is called a foot. A foot is a group of syllables forming a metrical unit. In English poetry, a foot contains a repetition of a combination of stressed and unstressed syllables. Depending on the stresses in a sentence, syllables are combined two or three at a time to create a foot, a basic rhythmical unit.

Examples:

Va BOOM is an iambic foot.
Va Va BOOM is an anapest.
BOOM Va   is a troche.

Meter

Meter is rhythm that continuously repeats a single basic pattern of feet. For example, Shakespeare used iambic pentameter, five feet of unstressed, then stressed syllables (five iambic feet in a row). According to Peter Meinke in *The Shape of Poetry,* "Establishing a basic meter helps the writer control the way a poem is read."

Read a poem aloud to capture its sound. If it doesn't sound pleasant to your ear or have the beat you want, check the meter.

Metaphor

A metaphor is an implied comparison between unlike things, saying one thing is another. Metaphors are similar to similes, but they are comparisons without using the words *like* or *as*.

Example from *Backpack Blues:*

Langdon Cross says, *You're a lifeline in a white apron.* What image does that bring to your mind? For any who have eaten in a school cafeteria, the picture is concrete, not abstract. Poets work for concrete images.

Chloe Hampton says, … *my life / is a crystal champagne flute."* Fragile?

Listen to Simon & Garfunkel's classic song, "I Am a Rock." How does the metaphor help you understand the lyrics? How is the image of a rock different from the image of a crystal champagne flute?

Can you find an extended metaphor in Martin Luther King Jr.'s famous "I Have a Dream" speech? Hint: You can take it to the bank.

Onomatopoeia

An easy form of figurative language is onomatopoeia. A word using onomatopoeia imitates the sound it makes. *Wham! The bat met the ball with a loud crack.*

Comic books and graphic novels are full of onomatopoeia. Pop! Bang!

Poets often use onomatopoeia. Example from "Casey Aro": "… *Crack / Crash!"*

Example from "Femi Thompson": You *snap* me like a fly at the end of your line.

Repetition

Say it again, Sam.

Lyricists repeat words, lines, stanza patterns, sentence structure, sounds, rhythms, and rhymes. Poets use repetition to add strength to their work. The rhythm of the repetition forms a musical beat.

Note the examples of repetition in *Backpack Blues*:

Check out "I do not wonder" from "Ysabel Gomez."

See "I'm a foster child—a hopeless stray" from "Leah Jones."

Think about your favorite song. Listen to the words and the music. Can you find examples of repetition?

Go back and listen to or reread Martin Luther King Jr.'s famous "I Have a Dream" speech. There are eight major units of repetition in his speech. Can you find them? Do you think they make the speech sound lyrical?

Rhyme

Rhyme is the repetition of similar sounds or the same sound in two or more words, most often in the final syllables of lines, but poets may attempt internal rhyme (rhyme between a word within a line and another word in the same line) or slant rhyme (almost rhyme).

Example of rhyming in "Mercedes Goldman," from this anthology:

> *She doesn't recognize goals I hold. / I must fit her chosen mold.*

Example of internal rhyme from "Ace Jackson":

> *Foul rumors spread like tumors.*

Rhyming is frowned upon in many circles today. Some consider it old-fashioned. I use it sparingly, most often in couplets and quatrains.

Rhythm

Rhythm is a poetic tool that demonstrates the long and short patterns of language through stressed and unstressed syllables. Listen for the measured movement or recurring sounds at regular intervals in poetry and music.

Shakespeare used iambic pentameter in most of his sonnets. In iambic pentameter, each line consists of ten syllables. Shakespeare's syllables are divided into five pairs, called iambs, or iambic feet. The iamb is a type of beat, or cadence, composed of one unstressed syllable followed by one stressed syllable. Say the word *good-bye* as you would in normal conversation. Notice *good* is unstressed (not emphasized). *Bye* is stressed (accented). Good-BYE. A line of iambic pentameter flows like this:

vaBOOM / vaBOOM / vaBOOM / vaBOOM / vaBOOM.

Forget poetry for a minute. Grab your earphones. Listen to a little modern music. Note the strong beat in rap or hip-hop music. How do the musicians use rhythm and rhyme to deliver a message in verse?

Note the rhyme and rhythm of the poetry forms discussed. Decide on the rhythm and rhyme that is right for each poem you write.

Sensory Words

Poets use sensory words. Can you remember studying the five senses? They are: taste, smell, touch, sight, and hearing. When poets use words that help us recall how something tastes, smells, or what it looks or feels or sounds like, they are using imagery, something that puts a picture in the reader's head.

Imagery

The use of words or groups of words to evoke associations —memories of what we've seen, smelled, tasted, felt, or heard is called imagery. Notice the use of a specific color.

Example from "Cora Simmons"
I cringe, / face warm and tomato-red.

Does it tell you what her face looked like?

From "Stormi Starr Stevens":

As for bullies, / the key to dealing with them / is to treat them like a / three-day-old tuna sandwich / left in some slob's stinky locker!

Can you smell the old fish?

Some words sound like their meanings. We see them on the page and we hear the sound they make. They appeal to our sense of hearing. (*See* onomatopoeia.)
Example:

My boyfriend, Terry Billings, says, /
Ka-ching! Ka-ching! Ka-ching!

Simile

A simile is a type of figurative language that is a direct comparison between two things that are unlike each other in most ways, but have one way they are similar. The comparison is introduced by the words *like* or *as*.
Example from "Paige Hacker":

From within, / my words surface like a mountain spring.

(Mountain springs don't usually originate with a gush. They begin with a trickle.)
A person's words are not like a mountain spring in most ways, but they both come up or out of something (a mouth, a crack in a mountain).
What does Leah Jones compare herself to? By the way, there's a literary allusion in the line. Can you find it? Think Carl Sandburg.

What does the line "We throw you like clay" in the "Marcus Cooper" poem say about how he treats women?

Personification

Personification is the giving of human qualities to an inanimate object or idea.

Examples from *Backpack Blues*:

> *Don't bother us; we're armed— / our trailer screams, offends, / and angers, fencing me in.*

Can an inanimate object like a trailer scream?

How is the line that follows, from "Ysabel Gomez," an example of personification? What inanimate object is given a human quality?

> *I watch their efforts to arrive at the fields early, / before the yellow sun sneaks over the skyline."*

Does the sun really sneak over the skyline? Does the description remind you of a daybreak you've witnessed?

Symbol

A symbol is something that stands for something else.

What do you associate with the color white? Why do brides wear white? Is it as pure as the driven snow, as the cliché indicates?

What are you saying about someone if you say he is *yellow*? What connotation does the term *yellow journalism* bring to mind? Is the connotation favorable, or does it remind you of fake news, a term popularized by President Donald Trump?

In *Backpack Blues*, do you get a clear understanding of what "Toby Tinker" means when he says, "He's insecure, grass-green jealous—"?

In the Sioux tradition, the color red symbolizes the East, the Great Spirit in the rising sun of life and light, and a new day born. When someone says, "I saw *red*," what meaning do you get from the color *red*?

Color is important to "Holly Meyers." Is there a color you prefer to wear? Do you want to drive a beige car? Why or why not?

Why do Goths wear black or other dark colors?

Hint: Did you know the term *gothic rock* was coined in 1967 by a music critic, to describe a meeting he had in a dimly lit wine cellar with the legendary lead singer of the Doors, Jim Morrison?

Does *dimly lit* give you an aha moment?

Color isn't the only symbol in *Backpack Blues*. What is Cora Simmons saying about herself when she says, "… to them I'm trailer girl— / too invisible to include"? Do trailers bring derogatory images to your mind? Are these stereotypes demeaning? Do you sympathize with Cora? Root for her?

Many of the names of the characters (poems) in *Backpack Blues* are symbols. For example, both Paige Hacker's first and last names are clues to the type of student she represents. There's a little poetic license with the spelling of the word *page*. What is a newspaper *hack*? If you didn't know, would you lose some of the subtlety in the character description?

Surprise

To make the most impact, a poem should surprise the reader. One good way to accomplish this is with a twist in the last stanza, couplet, or line.

How does the last line of "Melody Caroll" surprise the reader?

How does the last line of "Noah Newman" surprise the reader?

Locate and read Dorothy Parker's "Love Song" and "One Perfect Rose" to see how she uses humor and surprise to make her poetry memorable.

Florida poet laureate, Peter Meinke, uses surprise effectively in "Miss Arbuckle," which appears in his book, *The Shape of Poetry*. Please Google and read his humorous poem. Can you picture the teacher? *The Shape of Poetry* is a great book for aspiring poets. I highly recommend you read it.

Some Poems Follow a Blueprint.

One of my favorite poets, Amy Lowell, condemns patterns in her famous poem, "Patterns." She denounces war (which she calls a pattern). Her final question in the poem is: "What are patterns for?"

In most cases, I agree with Lowell's sentiment. I'm not one for blind conformity, but I steal what works for me from patterns and disregard what doesn't. I'm not in favor of following another's rules for poetry if the rules dampen my theme or intent. For the novice poet, working with a few poetry forms provides a firm foundation. For poets stuck in one mode, a pattern may provide a rebirth by challenging the writers to go beyond their comfort zones —to branch out into unfamiliar endeavors. Using a pattern forced me to leave my safety zone.

The form poem provides a blueprint for building a poem. During the revision process, keep what works and slash what doesn't.

Yes, I said revision process. Writers must jot down ideas as they come to mind, without worrying about spelling, punctuation, or structure. After the words are on the page, fine-tune them. I revise more than I compose.

I offer one quick note about punctuating poetry. Punctuate with purpose. There are no set-in-cement rules for poetry. No one can say exactly what is right or wrong, but an occasional punctuation mark is necessary to help the reader interpret the lines as the poet (you) intended. Punctuation marks also help the oral reader or slammer. Punctuation marks allow readers to pause and take a breath.

In the pages that follow, the reader will find a few types of poems to try. Try them all or try a few. Above all, keep in mind that good poets must read a variety of poems—traditional and contemporary—to find their niche or maybe even create a new form.

Types of Poems

Blues

Have you ever had the blues? How did you feel? Do any of your friends seem to go from blue to pink in a single week? What makes your friends blue? What makes you blue?

It was my intention for this eclectic collection of multicultural monologues to give voice to the angst, heartbreak, and dreams of students and their English teacher, creating a microcosm of one fictional high school class as I envisioned it based on students I taught, but never on any actual student. Do you feel your classmates' angst and heartbreak? Do some of your classmates struggle to fit into school society? Are there bullies and victims? Athletes and geeks?

Fluctuations in estrogen, progesterone, and testosterone—the sex hormones—result in teen mood swings. Have you noticed you're up one day and down the next? It's normal for teens to have the blues. That is one of the themes of *Backpack Blues*. Most teens have down days, yet they make it to the end of the day.

The blues is an American form, but its roots draw from African music. American blues trace back to the Deep South, originating as work songs and field hollers among slaves. One great example of a collection of early blues poetry is *Weary Blues* by Harlem Renaissance poet, Langston Hughes. Grab a copy and notice how the poet uses repetition of both language and rhythm.

Blues singers use repetition of lines, but often with slight variation. The last words of the first and fourth lines rhyme. Google and read Langston Hughes's "Morning After" and "As Befits a Man" to get a feel for blues poetry. Although it is normally serious, note how a blues poem can express the humor of a bad situation.

Blues songs deal with hopelessness, grief, and loss. Although they express the agony of life, they hint at the chance of conquering it through the same kind of toughness of spirit this anthology's "Janell Sparks" possesses. It's part of the American spirit. We may have rough times, but we rebound. We don't escape high school, but most move on to lead successful lives.

Blues poetry isn't concerned with formal grammar. It's more colloquial, everyday spoken language. *Ain't* finds its way into blues poetry and songs. Many blues songs begin with "Woke up this morning …" On some days, we may feel that's the best thing about the day, but for most of us, we're optimistic it's going to be a fresh beginning.

"Travis Indigo" is a blues poem and a blues song. Yes, you can turn your poetry into songs. Many popular music styles, including rhythm and blues, rock and roll, disco, rap, and jazz were drawn from the blues. Eric Clapton composed an album in memoriam of J. J. Cale's style of blues. By listening to *The Breeze: An Appreciation of JJ Cale*, Clapton's tribute, you may better understand the form. Another way to get the feel for the blues is to listen to a few traditional blues songs by Buddy Guy, Muddy Waters, Lightnin' Hopkins, and Blind Lemon Jefferson.

Notice the names? Blues names aren't politically correct. For men, they often include the name of a physical infirmity (weakness), or a first name plus the name of a fruit, or the last name of a president. Peg Leg Lime Clinton works. Little Willie would be a fine blues name, too. As for women, Sadie, Big Mama, and Bessie fit the blues mold.

Horrible stereotypes? That's traditional blues.

Setting is important in the blues. Good settings include the highway, the jailhouse, an empty bed, a Greyhound bus, a southbound train, or stuck in a ditch and ain't no way out.

You're on deck. Get the feel for the rhythm, loose rhyme, and the beat. Follow a pattern. In the sixteen-syllable first line, state the problem. Repeat the first line in the second line. In the third line, state half of the solution. The third and fourth lines should add up to sixteen syllables. In the fourth line, state the second half of the conclusion. Make sure the last word of the fourth line rhymes with the last word of the first line.

Now step up to the plate and write your blues poem. Think of something that depresses you. Typical subjects include: "I ain't got no money blues," "I wrecked my red Chevy blues," "Sitting by the dumpster blues," and "My mother's driving me crazy blues."

Luckily, high school students aren't always blue; however, most have enough problems to grumble and moan.

Blackjack

The most frequent type of poem in the *Backpack Blues* anthology is the blackjack poem. As I mentioned earlier, my friend and poetry mentor, Peggy Miller, introduced the form to me. My dad taught me to play the card game. In a blackjack card game, the perfect score is twenty-one. There are numerous ways to reach twenty-one, but an ace and a face card such as a king, queen, or jack most often produce winners (unless the dealer gets blackjack first). In the case of a tie, the dealer wins.

This relatively new form of poetry is based on that card game. It is called blackjack poetry because blackjack poems add up to twenty-one. The poems have three lines of seven syllables each. As mentioned previously, the Ace Jackson poem-stanza contains twenty-one syllables. Some have more than one twenty-one-syllable stanza. Did the "Ace Jackson" poems help to tie the *Backpack Blues* anthology together?

If you can count the syllables in words, you can create your own blackjack poem. Choose a topic and get started. Write the topic as your working title. Then compose three lines of seven syllables each about the topic. When you get to twenty-one, you have a poem.

If you want to change the title based on the content of the poem, go ahead and do so during the rewrite. Make any changes you want to the poem during your revising process, but just remember that a blackjack poem must have three lines of seven syllables each and must add up to twenty-one. If you end up with twenty-two lines, you're *busted*—the blackjack table's term for bankrupt—and what happened to Ace's father that made his mother leave him.

Sometimes I wrote two-stanza or three-stanza Ace Jackson poems. When I use more than one stanza, each stanza contains twenty-one syllables and each line contains seven syllables. Count the syllables in the first "Ace Jackson" poem. It reappears below:

ACE JACKSON

You call me the knave of hearts.
But listen to my gossip.
Foul rumors spread like tumors.

Note: Don't be concerned if Ace Jackson's poems confused you occasionally. Remember, Crosby Burney says Ace goes around mumbling twenty-one syllable poems. The information about him, his family, and his view about his classmates is revealed piecemeal, and he's troubled—not always clear.

Quatrain

Many people think poetry should rhyme. A good stanza form for those rhyming enthusiasts is the four-line quatrain. The length of the lines in quatrains may vary, but the second and last lines usually rhyme. A rare example of a quatrain in *Backpack Blues* is "Ruby O'Brien." Reread the short poem:

RUBY O'BRIEN

My hoverboard caught on fire.
That's why my homework is late.
Couldn't write—smoke in my eyes.
Don't blame me for what was fate.

I don't usually employ quatrains in my poetry, but ballad writers do. For a great example of a poem with quatrains, Google "The Ballad of the Harp-Weaver," by Edna St. Vincent Millay, or follow this link: https://www.poetryfoundation.org/poems/53241/the-ballad-of-the-harp-weaver.

Most of the stanzas in this touching poem are quatrains. Read the poem aloud and listen to the music of the verses about the miracle of a mother's love. Some of the poet's stanzas are five lines. Why do you think Millay varied the number of lines in her stanzas?

Beware: Rhyming poetry is considered outdated in many writing communities. In fact, at a recent conference, when I spoke of my novel in verse, a literary agent said, "It doesn't rhyme, does it?" His tone of voice and body language told me he wouldn't have looked at it if it did.

Your turn. Write a quatrain. If you wish, you can put two or more quatrains together and make a longer poem.

I-Am

The famous rock band, The Who, asked, "Who are you?" Answering that question is a great way to get to know the other members of a classroom or writing group. A fun and easy method to answer the question is in the form of a poem, the I-am poem. At first glance, the poem appears too simplistic to be an interesting piece, but, as you will see, it can be adapted.

The basic I-am or portrait poem begins with the pronoun *I* and a verb. In the eighteen-line I-am poem, some of the lines describe imaginary sights, sounds, and experiences. Other lines express what the poet has really experienced.

Let's write a poem. Begin by describing two characteristics or features about yourself, avoiding the obvious and the ordinary. Not *I am a fifteen-year-old girl with blonde hair*. How many fifteen-year-old blonde girls live in this country? A better first line appears in *Backpack Blues*: "I'm a spunky girl who loves gospel music." The line gives a sense of the speaker and how she might be different from other teens.

My I-am poem ends with a couplet. What's a couplet? Think of a couple. Two. Three's a crowd. Lines are coupled into pairs, and the paired lines must rhyme. I originally found this format in a *Scholastic* magazine. It is available in a number of places online.

Now you try it. Be as unique as you can be. Ready? Here's the big fat pitch. Take a swing at it. Go for a line drive, not a home run. Write your opening line and then shadow the line-by-line guide that follows, but break away from the pattern whenever you think you have an idea that will make the poem better if you step out of the pattern. When you finish writing your poem, go back and look at my poem titled, "Melody Caroll." Can you find where I stepped away from the blueprint? Did you like the changes? Did they make the poem stronger? Return to your poem and revise it. Wait a few days. Then go back and revise it again. Go for the home run. Be as creative as you can be.

Title –

Write your name or the subject of the poem
on a sheet of paper.

[First stanza]

I am (write two special characteristics you have)

I wonder (write something you are truly curious about)

I hear (a made-up sound)

I see (a fantasy sight)

I want (a genuine desire)

I am (the first line of the poem repeated)

[Second stanza]

I pretend (something you really pretend to do)

I feel (a feeling about something imagined)

I touch (an unreal touch)

I worry (something that actually bothers you)

I cry (something that makes you sad)

I am (the first line of the poem repeated)

[Third stanza]

I understand (something you know is a fact)

I say (something you believe in, especially when there
    is no absolute proof)

I dream (something you truly dream about)

I try (something you genuinely make an effort about)

I hope (something you really want more than anything
    else)

I am (part of the first line repeated, but do a little
    turnaround here. End with a word that rhymes with
    the last word of the previous line)

Reread "Asia Thomas" and "Melody Caroll."

Then, Google Maya Angelou's "Phenomenal Woman."
Read Miss Angelou's poem. What do you think of the power and
intensity in her poem? Go back to your poem. Could you tweak a
line or two to make your poem more powerful? Abandon the mold.

Google E. B. White's "Song of the Queen Bee." Read the poem. Note how he uses a little humor to comment on bees and society. Return to your poem. Could you add a speck of humor to make your poem better?

Musicians write I-am songs. Find and listen to Simon & Garfunkel's "I Am a Rock," or "I Am the Walrus," by The Beatles —or better yet, listen to both. "I Am a Walrus" is an example of an I-am poem, but it totally strays from the pattern. Do you want to change your poem, or are you ready to share it with your classmates?

I-Used-to-Be

Breathe a sigh of relief. The I-used-to-be poem is much shorter than the I-am poem. Through the use of symbols, the I-used-to-be poet tells the reader about a metamorphosis. Have you changed from a caterpillar to a butterfly, or from a toad to a prince? To write this poem, begin by thinking of two objects that could stand for you. One object should stand for the way you were when you were in grade school or before some traumatic or unusual event occurred in your life. The other item should represent the way you see yourself now.

Example:

> I used to be
> a sponge
> sucking in knowledge.
> But now I am
> a hornet stinging
> anyone who enters my path.

Ready to write? Follow these easy steps to write a one-or two-sentence I-used-to-be poem.

1. For the first line of the poem, write either *I used to be*, or *Once, I was*.
2. Write down the name of the object that best represents your former self.
3. Describe something about the object you just wrote that made it like you.
4. Next, either write *But now I am*, or *Now I am*. (If you write *But now I am*, you may not want to capitalize the *b* in *but*. Instead, you might want to put a comma at the end of the previous line and use the lowercase *b*. That depends on

whether you want a subordinate clause or a new sentence.) It's your poem. You decide, but do it during the revision process. Right now, just write the words, *But now I am* or *Now I am*.

5. In the next line, write down the object that represents you at this time in your life.
6. In one or two lines, describe something about this object that makes it seem like you.

Read what you wrote. Did you create a metaphor? What does it say about you? A characteristic of a good story is the transformation of a character. Hopefully, you have grown in your life. The I-used-to-be poem shows the change.

To change the "Chloe Hampton" poem to an I-used-to-be poem, you might pen the following lines:

I used to be
a champagne flute
sparkling in the limelight,
but now I am
a pile of shattered glass,
cutting all who touch me.

Is Chloe Hampton a prime subject for a blues poem? If you think so, challenge yourself to write her story in a blues poem. Then, go on to read about the two-tone poem. The two-tone poem is on deck.

Two-Tone

We've read about the blues. Have you ever heard someone say, "I'm feeling blue today"? What does that mean? Consider the mood of blues music. Please reread the "Travis Indigo" poem. How is the title symbolic of how a person feels after losing a pet?

According to psychologists, colors trigger certain feelings or moods in many people. For example, beige makes me feel blah. Some colors are *warm*. Others are *cool*. Babies' rooms are painted pastel colors. There was a time in the twentieth century when people paid to have their colors read, as some people pay to have their fortunes told. Color specialists recommended colors and the believers dressed in the colors that, according to the consultants, represented their personalities or made them look good.

Some colors attract attention. Other colors, like beige, blend in with their surroundings. What do you feel about colors? Do you have a color you love or hate? Did you ever think about why you chose the colors hanging in your wardrobe? Did you select the color of the paint on the wall in your bedroom? Is color important to you? Is there a color car you wouldn't want to drive? Why?

Armed with this knowledge, you can write an autobiographical poem. Read the following examples.

1. Part of me is vivid yellow
    lively and cheerful
    bouncy like a flashy sunflower
    joking with friends and loving the spotlight.

    But deep inside, I hide another side—
    pale purple, like a shy violet
    hiding under a dark green leaf—
    cowardly and self-conscious
    shaking when called to deliver my speech.
    Both colors are natural
    and they're both me.

2. Some days I'm tomato-red—
   ripe with energy and angry words,
   like a wildcat ready to spring.
   Other days I'm olive drab—
   scruffy, dull, and monotonous,
   lazy and worn-out like a favorite T-shirt.
   But stand back, frenemies,
   'cause today I'm red.

Reread these two formats suggested in *Your Turn: 33 Lessons in Poetry,* and then read my original poems based on this format. Which of the two poems above refers to two sides of a person's individuality or character? Which reveals or portrays the way a person's moods change from day to day?

Your turn at bat. Use either structure to write about your *two tones* (sides to your personality or different moods). Write your thoughts using poets' tools and original names for your colors, like blueberry blue or Christmas plaid.

After you have written, revised, and read the poem aloud, take two or more pieces of colored paper or colored pencils that illustrate your tones. Cut the paper into any shapes you like. Then attach the cutouts to your *two-tone poem* in appropriate places to suggest meaning. If you choose to use colored pencils, create a Zentangle (*see* Beckah Krahula's *One Zentangle a Day*) representation of your moods or personalities to illustrate the poem.

Poems can be visual as well as verbal. One type of poem, the concrete poem, is written in a shape that suggests its meaning. You might want to write one of your poems using that technique.

Life Metaphor

Have you ever seen the movie *Forrest Gump* or eaten at a Bubba Gump restaurant?

Do you remember how Forrest Gump's mother defined life? "Life is like a box of chocolates." How is it like a box of chocolates? Are you a life-is-a-bowl-of-cherries or a life-is-prison-bordered-with-barbed-wire-fences type of person? Let's revisit the poem, "Chloe Hampton."

CHLOE HAMPTON

I cry alone
   because my life
      is a crystal champagne flute
         shattered
           by the loss of
              boyfriend
              and
                  best friend in one
                    backstabbing—
                        Betrayal!

Is Chloe a pessimist, optimist, or a realist?

Life metaphor poems can define life, or, as I did in "Chloe Hampton," they can define what your life is or has been. Since you're the poet, you decide.

You're at bat with the bases loaded. Step up to the plate and write three poems defining life. Yes, it's like baseball. You get three swings. Write one poem from the point of view of an optimist, one from the point of view of a pessimist, and one from the point of view of a realist. Write each using an extended metaphor.

After you have written the poems, revise them. Prepare to read the one that best depicts your definition of life or your actual life. We should be able to tell if you are a pessimist, optimist, or realist, by listening to or reading your poem.

Fibonacci Poem

The Fibonacci (or Fib) poem, named for Leonardo Pisano (also known as Fibonacci), an Italian mathematician, is a great poem for mathematic-minded writers. The Fib poem is a multiple-line verse based on the Fibonacci sequence. The key to writing this poem is to count the number of syllables in each line of the poem. The number of syllables in each line equals the total number of syllables in the previous two lines.

The Fibonacci sequence begins with either zero or one, followed by one, and continues based on the rule that each number equals the sum of the preceding two numbers. Since the lines have ever-increasing syllables, the long Fibonacci poem is challenging for the average student, but popular with geeks. I bet Noah Newman could write one. For those of us who aren't geeks, most of our Fibonacci poems are no more than six or seven lines long.

Pisano found examples of this poetry form used in Sanskrit poetry, as far back as the twelfth century, but others believe it goes back to BC. Re-read the following poem from *Backpack Blues*:

WILLOW PISANO

Pain
Slit
Abuse
Rejection
I recall each wound
A bangle of tears mars my wrist

Is it a Fibonacci poem? What is the significance of the title? Is it too lame? I challenge you to come up with a better title.

Now it's your turn. Try a Fibonacci poem. Challenge yourself. How many lines can you write without losing the sequence? Does your poem make sense? How does it sound to your ear when you read it aloud? It is important to read aloud any poem or story you write before sharing it with others. If you do, you may find places where it sounds disjointed or awkward. If so, rework the lines.

Acrostic Poem

Acrostic poems are super easy poems to write. To write an acrostic poem, spell a word down the side of a piece of paper vertically. Use boldface print. Begin with something easy, like your name, favorite sport, or hobby. The letters of the word you wrote vertically become the first letter of the lines of the poem.

In the example poem titled "Melody" that follows, I use the letters of my first name.

MELODY

Melody
Eats
Loneliness, longing, and love
Overweight
Diabetic
Yields to basic desires.

Can you see the name written vertically as the starting line of the poem? Go back and read the "Toby Tinker" poem. What problem do "Melody" and "Toby Tinker" share?

The poet may write the same word or phrase more than once and get more stanzas. The poem "Runaway Pond" in this collection is an acrostic poem. Notice that the word *Runaway* is repeated to allow the poet to say everything she wants to say about the Vermont pond. In the last stanza, the word *Run away* becomes two words to tell what the girl Celine is doing. This startles the reader who, up until the last stanza, considers the poem to be about a place, not a person. Surprise! To keep the reader interested, your poetry anthology should be one big surprise party.

Repeating-Line

Do your parents, teachers, or friends have a favorite statement they tend to use routinely? Would you like to respond to the line, but don't want to get into trouble for *talking back*? Or do you have a line you say many times every week? That line could be a great taking-off point for what is known as the repeating-line poem. In the repeating-line poem, you write the line that is often repeated and respond to it.

In case you are having trouble thinking of frequently repeated lines, I have listed a few lines former students mentioned. Hopefully, the list will, in the words of the Daytona 500 starter, "Start your engines."

"As long as you're living under my roof …"
"Because I said so …"
"If you don't turn that cell phone off, it's going to be
        mine."
"Don't wait until the last minute."
"Turn down the TV."
"Don't text and drive."
"Who else is going to be at the party?"
"What did you learn today?"
"Have you done your homework yet?"
"You're old enough to know better."
"Put your phone away at the table."
"Money doesn't grow on trees."
"Get a job."
"I hope you have a kid just like you."
"Do you think I just fell off the turnip truck?"
"Whatever …"
"Awesome …"
"There are things growing in your room."
"Save your money."

"I don't care what everybody else is doing."
"You're grounded."
"You're not wearing that out of this house."
"You're not wearing that to school."
"Say what?"
"#MeToo."

Go back and read the poems titled "Suki Tan" and "Melanie Andrews" in this collection. They are examples of the repeating-line poem; but as you can see, I took a little poetic license, changing the form to meet my needs. You can do the same. Poetic license gives the poet the freedom to disobey rules.

Try it out. Write the repeated word or phrase as the title of your poem. For the first line of the poem, write the word or phrase again. Then respond to the word or phrase. Continue alternating lines between the word or phrase and your response until you have said everything you wanted to say to make your point.

When you have finished writing the poem, read it aloud. Revise if it doesn't sound good to your ear. Then share it with a friend, teacher, or classmate.

Chant

Chant poems are repeating-line poems. The word *chant* comes from a Latin word meaning *song*. It is believed that cavemen and women sat around the fire chanting to protect themselves from wild animals, hurricanes, and fires, and to give themselves an advantage in the hunt for food and a mate. Have you ever heard the cheerleaders for your favorite team in a chant? Are cheerleaders' chants designed to give their team luck and support? Does it help the team to have a cheerleader? "Charlotte Emo" is a chant poem. In an interview on *Face the Nation*, Jon Batiste, *The Late Show with Stephen Colbert* bandleader, said his new rendition of "The Battle Hymn of the Republic" is part chant. Listen to it to find the chant.

As with the other repeating-line poems you wrote, the key to writing a good chant is to select a good line you want to repeat. The repeated line is the foundation of the poem. A good line will have a cadence (tempo), or beat, that seems musical to your ear. Before attempting to write a chant, go online and listen to a few blues songs, slave songs, and prison work songs. They draw from the chant format. Do some popular songs repeat and/or chant?

You're in the on-deck circle. Time to consider what you have in your equipment bag.

Since chants have an openness and spontaneity not found in sonnets or quatrains, just plunge into the opening lines without predetermining what your beginning, middle, or end will be. Combine repeated lines and phrases with words and sentences that vary, like a good pitcher's pitches. Don't forget that the element of surprise is as important to the poet as it is to the pitcher.

Epistle

An epistle (from the Latin word for *letter*) is a poem that is also a letter to someone. The tone and substance of an epistle depend on the person it is directed to. Letters to friends and relatives sound different from letters to employers, business associates, and senators.

For traditional examples, Google Alexander Pope's "Epistle to Dr. Arbuthnot" or "Dear Mama," by Langston Hughes. One of my favorite epistles isn't really a letter at all. It's a short note like we might stick on the refrigerator. The title of this little epistle by William Carlos Williams is "This Is Just To Say." Find the poem. Read it. Then read what the critics say it means.

Read "The Passionate Shepherd to His Love" by Christopher Marlowe.

Please go back to "Ethan Stafford" in *Backpack Blues*. Do you understand the poem better? Do you agree with Ethan?

Locate "Mother to Son," by Langston Hughes. It's a wonderful example of a poem addressing someone. This is a variation of the epistle.

Epistles can be written to real or invented (fictional) people. "An Epistle to My Sister" and "Shannon Traynor" in this book are both epistles.

Do you have someone you would like to say something to, but you never have the nerve to say it? As the cliché goes, do you *chicken out*? Your turn to get it off your chest is now. Write a poem in the form of a letter. Say what you want to say. For a fun follow-up activity, write a poem in response to the original epistle, as Sir Walter Raleigh does in his "The Nymph's Reply to the Shepherd," in response to "The Passionate Shepherd to His Love" by Christopher Marlowe.

Insult

Is it time to do some dissing? Ever heard statements like, "Your momma wears combat boots" or "You aren't exactly the ace in the card deck"? Statements like these can lead to insult poems. Like chants, they repeat lines, but these lines aren't concerned with basic forces like love, hatred, or the weather. Insult poems get personal, telling the person some truths about themselves. (Of course, these truths are in the speaker or writer's opinion.) Insult poems use humor and exaggeration and allow one to show off verbal skills and demonstrate one's superiority with words, not fists. Think of the "Drop the Mic" segment of James Corden's *The Late Show*. Wouldn't it be nice if our diplomats could use words to demonstrate our country's superiority so our armed forces didn't have to spend so much time at war? As "Troy Rush" would say, "Just an innocent little question ..." to let you know my opinion about war.

Ever heard of playing the Dozens to exchange insults in a verbal battle? In playing the Dozens, two competitors (usually males), go head-to-head in a competition of trash talk, taking turns *cracking on*, or *insulting*, one another or the adversary's mother or sister, until there is no comeback. For a deeper understanding of insult poems, check out woofin', wolf ticket, and signifyin'.

Rap

Rap poetry is, first and foremost, an oral form. *Rap* means to talk. A rap artist's pitch is meant to convince listeners that the ideas presented in the rap are valuable and that the person presenting them is *cool*.

Traditionally, rap contained tapping and clapping sounds or *mouth music*, a rhythmic beat created by making sucking, popping, and clicking sounds with the mouth and hands in the background. Today, rappers create rhythm by using an electronic background. Roll your windows down when passing through a big city, and you're likely to hear the rapper's heavy bass. Maybe you can even feel the vibrations.

A good regular rap has four accented beats per line and, performed aloud, contains about 130 beats per minute. A crucial element to making rap work is the tone of the rapper's voice. Listen for the tone to go from loud to soft. Since raps are usually stories about life in the inner city, the artists typically season the lyrics with ultra-contemporary slang in order to realistically depict street life, hard times, drugs, or personal relationships.

Like insult poems, rap has its origins in the African oral traditions that traveled across the Caribbean and the antebellum (pre–Civil War) South. It appears to have grown from *signifying*, a type of rhyming insult contest. The *signifying monkey*, a wily trickster character of the monkey (with more brain than brawn) who opposes bigger, stronger, but duller foes, is said to be the basis of the rap form. According to this theory, the rapper is the monkey-warrior fighting his or her enemies with word magic. At times, the pacifist in me wishes we could all use words rather than guns to fight, but words can also hurt deeply, can't they?

In *Backpack Blues* the characters refer to rap music and rap musicians, but there are no rap poems. Why? The setting is the rural Adirondack region of New York State, about three hundred miles north of New York City. Most of the characters have never witnessed inner-city problems. They deal with problems that country kids face. Loneliness, alienation, teen pregnancy, bulimia and anorexia nervosa, and bullying are facts of life, but usually, not gang violence.

If you want to write rap, listen to rap musicians. Notice that rap is based on groups of four. The drum pattern is kick, snare, kick, snare. The rhyming words in rap normally fall on beat four, the second snare. If, like me, you aren't a musician, you might be asking, what's a snare? A snare is a type of drum. A characteristic of its sound is its short and sharp smack or slap. There are four beats in each bar. Typically, the first and third beat sounds are made on the kick drum, the bass drum played using a pedal. The second beat and fourth beats come from the snare drum.

To learn to write rap songs, do a Google search. A number of YouTube tutorials will come up on your screen. Watch a few. Then write your rap. Be sure you have a story to tell. Put the words to the beat. Did you know rappers were originally called emcees, not rappers? Emcees serve as hosts at such functions as presidential roasts, the Oscars, and the Grammys. The term stands for *master of ceremonies*. Sometimes, *emcee* is spelled *MC* as in *DMC* (digital mixing console). As stated previously, in *Backpack Blues*, Ace Jackson serves the function of a master of ceremonies. The members of some rap groups take turns with the vocals rather than have one lead singer do all the singing, but most groups have a lead singer or emcee.

Pay attention as you listen to your favorite rap song. Notice that some of the end rhymes don't rhyme unless you pronounce them in a certain way. This type of rhyme scheme is called *slant rhyme*. Avoid forced rhyme. In other words, do not change the structure of your line or stanza to make something rhyme.

Play rap music loudly (but don't overdo it) when you can get away on your own. Wear headphones. Absorb the beat. When your body becomes a musical instrument resonating with rap rhythms, you're ready. Choose a point (theme) you want to make. Start to tell it aloud to yourself, your cat, and your dog. Try it out on a friend. If you get stuck on some rhymes and tricky parts, go back and work on them. When you have the rhythm, words, rhymes, and beats in your head and body, get them on paper. Then go back. Rap artists like Jay-Z and Eminem use couplets. As you revise, add couplets and internal rhyme. Practice reading your rap until you own the beat. Do you need a change-up to make the rap more interesting? As the pitcher throws a change-up pitch to surprise the batter, throw the reader a little unexpected twist in the ending couplet.

Can you catch the couplet in these two lines? Watch for the end rhyme.

> Your creative session has come to an end.
> It's time to share your poem with a friend.

You can do better. Now share raps with friends. Present your rap orally. Put it to music if you can.

Pantoum

The pantoum is composed of multiple quatrains. The second and fourth lines of the previous stanza are repeated in the stanza that follows. This pattern continues until the last stanza. The final quatrain breaks from the repetitive outline. The third line of the last stanza is the second line of the first quatrain. The last line of the poem repeats the first line of the poem. "Femi Thompson" began as an example of a modern version of the pantoum; however, I added one line to the end of the poem to modernize it.

This verse form follows a definite blueprint, or pattern, of repetitive lines. Each stanza contains four lines. They don't have to rhyme. To review, the second and fourth lines of each stanza are repeated as the first and third lines of the next stanza, until the last stanza. In the last stanza, the first and third lines are the second and fourth of the stanza above. The last line is a repeat of the first line of the poem, and the third line of the first stanza is the second line of the last stanza. Note how repetition moves the pantoum forward and quickens the poem's pace.

The pantoum pattern looks like this:

Line one
Line two
Line three
Line four

Line five (repeat of line two)
Line six
Line seven (repeat of line four)
Line eight

[Continue with:]
Line two of previous stanza
Line three of first stanza
Line four of previous stanza
Line one of the first stanza

127

Since I don't like to stick to a pattern all the time, I added a final line, so the "Femi Thompson" poem isn't a true pantoum. Would you prefer the poem without the last line, or does the last line modernize it?

The pantoum sounds confusing, but is actually fun. Use "Femi Thompson" and the format above as your guide, and write a pantoum. Stick strictly to the pattern or deviate from it. Revise and share, or if you prefer, go to https://www.poemhunter.com/poem/pantoum-3/. Many consider John Ashbery's poem titled "Pantoum" to be an excellent example of a pantoum. I find Ashbery's poem difficult to relate to, but his form is perfect. I prefer Donald Justice's "Pantoum of the Great Depression." Why not read both? Which do you prefer? Locate Justice's pantoum by clicking here: https://www.poetryfoundation.org/poems/58080/pantoum-of-the-great-depression.

Narrative Poem

It has been said that everyone loves a good story. In contrast to lyric poems, which appeal to the emotions, narrative poems tell a story. Many readers compare them to prose.

Have you ever heard or read "The Cremation of Sam McGee," by Robert W. Service? If not, find and read this unique narrative. Another fun narrative poem is "Casey at the Bat," by Ernest Lawrence Thayer. If you like sports and have not read "Casey at the Bat," you owe yourself the opportunity to read it. These works are great examples of narrative poems.

In 1915, Edgar Lee Masters published a collection of poems titled *Spoon River Anthology*. His poems gave voice to the dead in his fictional town, named after the real Spoon River near his home. Masters allows the dead to gossip about each other and discuss the injustices, insults, and indignations they faced while alive, using symbolism in the names to reflect the characters he portrays.

The seed of my book of narrative poems grew from class discussions of Masters's *Spoon River Anthology*. I witnessed pain, humiliation, hopes, and alienation. Like the Mrs. Deyon in my collection, I received poems and essays revealing secrets and angst. I asked myself, *Why not let teens know that they are not alone in their fears and alienation?*

I jotted down the stories I heard in the halls, the stories students shared, and the events that unfolded in the classroom. One poem at a time, one problem at a time, one hurt at a time, the poems began to take shape. After my thoughts and themes were on paper, I started the process of revising, making sure never to use real names or totally true descriptions. At that time, I decided to experiment with a variety of formats.

If a poem tells a story, it is a narrative poem. Write the story you want to share. Are there unique characters in your school or town? What's their story? What's your story? Write it. Try writing your poems from both the first and third person. Which person works better for the story you want to tell?

Lyric

Lyric poetry expresses emotions, thoughts, and feelings. A lyric poem is a short poem that conveys the poet's thoughts and emotions in a musical style. In ancient Greece, lyric poets wrote poems to be sung, accompanied by a lyre. Today we call the words to a song *lyrics.*

Musical lyrics are frequently love poems put to music, but musicians may express an array of emotions.

Most lyric poems use personal pronouns such as *I, we,* and *our.* Sonnets, elegies, and odes are examples of lyric poetry. Since love is an emotion, love poems are generally lyric poems.

According to the February 22, 2010, issue of *Scholastic Action,* when singer Taylor Swift won Album of the Year at the 2009 Country Music Awards, she said, "This album is my diary. Thank you for saying that you like my diary." She added, "If you break my heart, hurt my feelings, or mess with my friends, I will write a song about you."

Do you write about your feelings in a diary? It is my greatest writing regret that I did not keep a diary. Sometimes it's hard to recapture the feelings we had at the time of a significant moment in our lives.

I write to disclose reasons for student angst and to let teens know they are not alone with their feelings. Others may be going through similar difficulties. If you hurt teens, I'll expose you in my poems. I write to right. Since I don't write music, I stick to lyric and narrative poems. If you know music, you may want to write your poems as songs.

Lyric poets write about more than love. Their writing depicts passion, anger, loss, despair, loneliness, heroes, dreams, injustice, spring, nature, mothers, fathers, innocence, marriage, and death—the topics are endless.

Dr. George Abbe, my first creative writing teacher at the State University of New York in Plattsburgh, recommended we reach deep into the recesses of our minds for inspiration. He told us to write about memories from many years before the time of our writing and to give events time to process. He said, "The longer you have lived with it, the better." Dr. Abbe added, "The natural material for writing, then, must be authentic, personal experience, and as far back as possible—in spite of the universals that are also important—different."

Ephesians 4:26–27 reads: "In your anger do not sin." It might be best not to write in the heat of the moment, either. When written upon reflection, our poems, essays, and songs may better capture the whole truth, rather than just the anger. However, many turned to poetry immediately after the September 11 tragedy. It would be interesting to see if their poems would be more powerful if those same poets wrote about the tragedy today after years of reflection.

At first reading, one of our nation's most famous lyric poets, William Wordsworth, appears to disagree with Dr. Abbe. Wordsworth called poetry "the spontaneous overflow of powerful feelings." He added, "It takes its origins from emotions recollected in tranquility." Thus, it is not contradictory.

Modern instructors would probably say write organically.

As I told you earlier, many of my ideas come to me in the peacefulness of the night or the serenity of the bathtub or shower. If you're stuck on the wording for a poem or story, find your quiet spot to relax and inspiration may come, or sleep on it.

My first recollection of a poetry assignment in grade school was to memorize and deliver a poem to the class. We were given a list of poems to choose from. None of the poems meant anything to me until I saw "I Wandered Lonely as a Cloud," sometimes referred to as "Daffodils," by Wordsworth. I related to daffodils because they are the flower for the month of March—my birth month.

Since my mother often put daffodils on the table for my birthday dinner and I love relaxing on my back gazing at clouds, in my ignorance I decided to memorize Wordsworth's lyric poem "Daffodils." This poem, written in the early 1800s, is considered Wordsworth's most famous romantic poem. Once I got beyond the clouds and daffodils, though, it meant very little to my fifth-grade mind. My inability to relate to the poem made it difficult to memorize.

Wordsworth teamed with Samuel Taylor Coleridge to write *Lyrical Ballads, with a Few Other Poems.* Wordsworth wrote poetry designed to transform the daily drama of ordinary people into art. His co-author, Coleridge, was assigned the task of going beyond the ordinary, to the wildest flights of the imagination. He did just that.

In *Lyrical Ballads* Wordsworth gave beauty to simple and commonplace things like nature and spring, even a skylark. In contrast, Coleridge, like Edgar Allan Poe, evoked an atmosphere of mystery, wonder, and suffering. If you like Poe, I think you'll like Coleridge.

The romantic Coleridge wrote "Kubla Khan" about a palace that came to him in a dream. Hooked on dreams? I highly recommend you read "Kubla Khan." Note how he uses rhyme, alliteration, and assonance. Does the poem stimulate your imagination? Notice how he uses powerful imagery and common language.

Coleridge also wrote "The Rime of the Ancient Mariner." It's one of my favorite poems combining elements of lyricism and narration. Like *Princess Bride*, it's a frame story, starting in the present, flashing back to the past, and returning to the present. Most lyric poems do not tell a story. For that reason, "The Rime of the Ancient Mariner" might also be considered a narrative poem or a ballad by some, including me. Although it appears in *Lyrical Ballads*, it is more of a ballad with powerful descriptions and emotional force than a lyric poem.

Most of the stanzas have four lines (quatrains), with the second and fourth lines rhyming. However, not all stanzas stick to the four-line ballad form. Coleridge didn't sacrifice meaning to stick to the four-line ballad form. Never sacrifice meaning to stick to a formula. Poets own poetic license.

"The Rime of the Ancient Mariner" has worked its way into our language. When you see in how many ways, you may decide you want to read it. For example, have you ever heard someone call something "an albatross around my neck"? Recently, on Facebook, a former student said, "We sold the house. It was an albatross around our necks." I wondered if she remembered where the line originated. The albatross is a bird important to Coleridge's theme. Want to know what happens to the albatross? Read the poem.

Another famous line from the poem is "Water, water, everywhere / Nor any drop to drink." Have you heard it before? If so, what were the circumstances?

My favorite line is: "As idle as a painted ship / Upon a painted ocean." What image comes to your mind? Does Coleridge's use of simile and alliteration make it easy for you to picture a painted ship upon a painted ocean?

Many lyric poems are written from the first person. Read "We Real Cool" by Gwendolyn Brooks. Does the first person make it more personal? Believable?

Were you able to relate to any Emily Dickinson poems? Her "A Narrow Fellow in the Grass" captures the feelings I get when I encounter a snake.

Want to understand issues many women have strong feelings about? Read Marge Piercy's "Rape Poem" and Maya Angelou's "Phenomenal Woman." Why might women in the #MeToo movement champion "Rape Poem"? How is Maya Angelou's "Phenomenal Woman" empowering?

After my students had read "Phenomenal Woman," a number of the girls printed it out and taped it in their lockers or tacked it on their bulletin boards.

When I think of modern odes, Gary Soto's "Ode to Pablo's Tennis Shoes" comes to mind. What do your sneakers say about you? What would you like to say to them?

Your turn. Try your hand at writing a lyric poem. Write about something for which you have strong feelings. Use the first person. Will you write about a flower, tree, love, or your sneakers? Put it aside for a couple days. Try the same poem in the third person. Which version do you prefer?

Found Poem

Found poems are exactly what one would expect them to be. The poet creates a poem by finding words, phrases, or even whole passages from other sources and reframing the words as poetry. The writer of the found poem finds words in a newspaper, piece of literature, ads, phone books, or other sources, and makes changes in spacing and lines, and adds or deletes text to create new meaning. Found poems are the literary equivalent of a collage.

A teacher in Deltona, Florida, asks her students to write spine poems. She takes them on a field trip to the library. Students select a couple of books with titles of interest to them—titles that speak to their hearts. Then they choose another four to six books with interesting titles. Step three is to pile the books into a stack. In the fourth step, students revise by swapping the order of the book spines. The teen poets explore how the meaning changes when the order changes. They work until they are content the poem not only make sense when the titles are read from the top to the bottom, but also has significance to them. Finally, they snap a picture of the pile, and a poem is born. No writing required!

In a variation of spine poetry, students write the title of a book or song in a vertical line, providing the spine, or backbone, of the poem. Students are free to write about almost anything, but each line must start with a word from the title they found. The spine poem combines aspects of the found poem and the acrostic poem. A very simple spine poem follows.

The Bait Man
By D. L. Havlin

The lonely orphan girl is
Bait for the predatory
Man lurking in the shadows.

I rarely write found poems, but I combined the rules for the found poem and the sestina to write a found poem for the NEA's (National Endowment for the Arts) Great Gatsby Big Read, sponsored by Volusia County, as part of the DeBary, Florida, program. It was quite a challenge, and I took a little poetic license in the final tercet (a set, or group, of three lines of verse rhyming together or connected by rhyme with an adjacent tercet). My *Great Gatsby* found sestina follows the explanation of the sestina.

Sestina

In his first inaugural address, President Franklin D. Roosevelt said, "… the only thing we have to fear is fear itself." I'm not sure that's true, since I suffer from ophidiophobia and there are snakes slithering all around Florida. Just as my fear of snakes cripples me, my fear of failure (atychiphobia) kept me from attempting to write a sestina. Like all cowards, I gave up without making an effort. After sending the first few pages of my poetry to be critiqued, I became brave. I studied the form, read Elizabeth Bishop's poem, "Sestina," and wrote six words on a page.

Now I'm hooked on sestinas. Unlike many terse poems, the thirty-nine-line sestina gives the poet the opportunity to explore a subject or theme in depth. The form provided the avenue I needed for my poetry book to touch on the reality of the human trafficking of runaways.

The sestina form contains six unrhymed stanzas of six lines each, followed by a three-line tercet, or *envoi* (French for *sending away*). The last words of the first six lines reappear at the ends of all the other lines and in the coda, a three-line tercet. The coda serves to round out, or conclude, the poem. Think of the sestina as an engine, with each stanza that follows a boxcar, followed by a caboose. Please reread my first poem in *Backpack Blues*, titled "Jane Dove," to get a feel for the form.

One reason I like the sestina is it alleviates the *need* some poets have to force rhymes.

Let's begin. Choose six words to be your end words. Aim for words that have multiple meanings or that evoke a mood, place, or season. Place the chosen words in each stanza in the order listed.

1 2 3 4 5 6
6 1 5 2 4 3
3 6 4 1 2 5
5 3 2 6 1 4
4 5 1 3 6 2
2 4 6 5 3 1
(6 2) (1 4) (5 3)

My sample sestina is below.

A Sestina "Found" in the Pages of *The Great Gatsby*

Over the ash heaps the giant **eyes**
Voices and color under the constantly changing **light**
Halfway between West Egg and New **York**.
"Make us a cold drink," cried **Daisy**.
"Gatsby?" demanded Daisy. "What **Gatsby**?"
"I can't say anything in his house, old **sport**."

"I don't trust him, old **sport**."
You perceive after a moment the **eyes**.
"Shall we go in my car?" suggested **Gatsby**.
A tray of cocktails floated at us through the twi**light**.
I wonder where in the devil he met **Daisy**.
He's quite a character around New **York**.

"I got here a minute ago, from New **York**."
"How surprised I was to find out I loved her, old **sport**."
He hadn't once ceased looking at **Daisy**.
Looked at Gatsby with unmoved **eyes**.
Brass button on her dress gleamed in the sun**light**.
"We've met before," muttered **Gatsby**.

"We'll all come over to your next party, Mr. **Gatsby**.
Tom's got some woman in New **York**.
You always have a green **light**."
"It's the funniest thing, old **sport**."
"But there was no laughter in his **eyes**."
"I'll say it whenever I want to! **Daisy**!"

"It couldn't be helped!" cried **Daisy**.
"Oh, you want too much!" she cried to **Gatsby**.
A bewildered look came back into his faded **eyes**.

Plunging home through the rain from New **York**.
"Don't you call me old **sport**."
"Gatsby believed in the green **light**."

"Drove on toward death through the cooling twil**ight**."
"We haven't met for many years," said **Daisy**.
"Loved each other all that time, old **sport**."
"Your wife doesn't love you," said **Gatsby**.
"She ran out there an' the one comin' from N'**York**."
Saw with a shock that he was looking at the **eyes**.

"A single green light—preyed on **Gatsby**.
Was Daisy driving when we left New **York**?
You must remember, old sport, to avoid all **eyes**."

The six words I chose are important to *The Great Gatsby*, but a person who has not read the book recently would probably have a great deal of trouble understanding my sestina. Therefore, it violates my rule for teaching poetry to teens or others who dislike poetry. I bet you could do a better job of writing a sestina. Choose your favorite book. Write six words from the book. Write a sestina. Don't narrow yourself to sentences the writer used, but use six words you find in the book, or better yet, choose six words that deal with you and your life.

By the way, some poems don't end up in a collection. This sestina is an example of a form, but it isn't worthy of inclusion in the poetry section. I struck out with this poem, but I'll write more poems. After a catastrophe, pick yourself up and start over again. If you're an athlete or even watched a baseball or softball game, you know not even the greats like Babe Ruth, Mickey Mantle, Ted Williams, and Aaron Judge hit every ball out of the park.

Abecedarian

Wow! Abecedarian sounds scary, doesn't it? Well, if you have a little time to spare, the abecedarian poem is a super-easy poem to write. An abecedarian poem is another acrostic form. Begin by writing the alphabet down the left side of the page, and then fill in the poem, or if you want, begin with the letter *Z* and go backward to the *A* and fill in the lines of the poem. The abecedarian poem is guided by the alphabet and is often used as a mnemonic device to teach children.

The letters of the alphabet must be in order. In another variation of the alphabet poem, the poet uses a few letters of the alphabet in order, but doesn't necessarily begin with the letters *A* or *Z*. Those poems aren't twenty-six lines long.

I wrote an alphabet poem for the NEA Great Gatsby Big Read, combining my knowledge of the book, history, and family. It follows.

The Decade Roared

Amendment 18 passed and Aunt Alvita died in a
    bootlegging hit-and-run accident.
Bobbed hair, blues, Bobby Jones, and baseball's Babe
    emerged.
Charlie Chaplin was The Little Tramp; the
    Charleston, the dance; Coolidge, the president.
Designers like Coco Chanel created styles making simple
    clothes chic.
Expatriate writers like Hemingway, Stein, and Fitzgerald
    became the "Lost Generation."
Fun, fragrance, and frolics pleased floozies and flappers
    dancing to fascinatin' rhythms.
Gatsby, a fictional rags-to-riches character, won
    acclaim for writer Fitzgerald.
Hotels opened tea salons for patrons taking afternoon tea,
    and Herbert Hoover elected.

It girl Clara Bow with her cupid-bow lips, topped the box-
office hit list.

Jolson, jazz, "Jackrabbit" Johnnie Dillinger, and Jack
Dempsey rose to the forefront, while

King (Joe) Oliver's Creole Jazz Band welcomed Satchmo,
a.k.a. Louis Armstrong.

Liberated women, luxuries, and Lindbergh brought
adventure to the masses.

Mafia gangsters like Al Capone burst into speakeasies,
shattering the night with gunfire.

New Orleans, the Big Easy, started the party, but
New Yorkers also swayed and stomped.

Ocean cruises required clothes sporting nautical
motifs. Anchors aweigh!

Prohibition ushered in mob rule, bootleggers, and
bathtub gin.

Queen of the Blues, Bessie Smith, dubbed the Empress of
the Blues.

Ringling Brothers carried the Greatest Show on Earth to
towns across the country.

Sacco and Vanzetti, working-class Italian-American
immigrants: martyred or murdered?

Treasures from the tomb of Tutankhamen led to the
Egyptian revival in accessories.

Untouchable Eliot Ness destined to become a movie hero.

Vanzetti and Sacco condemned to death and Millay and
Dos Passos penned poems.

Women wore dropped, loose-waistline dresses, waved or
bobbed their hair, and voted.

Xenophobia caused by the influx of immigrants spawned
the Ku Klux Klan.

"**Y**es Sir, That's My Baby," "Ain't We Got Fun," and "
You've Got a Kissable Mouth" resonated.

Zany Zelda Sayre married F. Scott Fitzgerald, and
they lived in a world gone wrong.

I'm sure you can come up with an alphabet poem. Try it. This one doesn't please me. Before you write your abecedarian poem, you might want to read "The ABC of Aerobics" by Peter Meinke. It's a better example.

Dramatic Monologue

When I began writing this collection of poems, the intent was to create all dramatic monologues, also known as *persona* poems. The audience was to be implied: other students, teachers, parents, and citizens of the school and town. There wasn't a plan for dialogue. As the poet, I planned to speak through the assumed voice of each of the characters—fictional students—communicating the feelings of the characters through their words. I needed to put on a figurative mask and become a teen.

How often did I succeed? Have any of the poems retained this format through the various revisions?

"Diego Vasquez" is an intended departure for two reasons. A few students prefer paired-partner poems, employing dialogue. Secondly, since my hope is for students to read their poems aloud and some students are uncomfortable delivering speeches, the partner in the paired-partner, or dialogue, poem provides a sense of security.

Can you do it? Challenge yourself to give voice to three people you've met who seem to be suffering in silence or festering under the skin. Is there a perpetual victim in your school? Is there a homeless person everybody seems to walk by and never really notice, or to taunt if they do notice him or her? Is there a quirky person you've seen often, but don't interact with? Is there an older or younger teacher who is a little eccentric? Is your minister out of touch or in touch with young people? Does your town have a character everybody knows, but nobody understands? What would your mom, dad, sister, or brother say if they were given the opportunity to tell people what it's really like, being them? What secret are you holding back? What is it like being you? What does no one else know?

Write three to five names on a sheet of paper. Do not use real names. Create names that give hints as to the personality or physical description of the person. Then, write lines to let each character speak. Give the character voice—his or her voice, not yours, except in the poem about you. Say what the character wants you to say, not what you want to say about the character.

As Atticus Finch tells his daughter, Scout, in *To Kill a Mockingbird*, get in the character's skin. Walk a mile in his or her shoes. By the way, to make it real, before you begin writing, decide what type of shoes the character will be wearing: sneakers, flip-flops, cowboy boots, worn-out dance slippers, stilettos, sandals, wedges, combat boots, wing tips, Jimmy Choos, pumps, Crocs, mules, rope, saddle shoes, or flats. What type of outfit? Will he or she be stylish or frumpy?

I pictured Cora Simmons in a frumpy outfit, wearing old-fashioned tennis shoes. How did you picture her?

To improve the imagery, draw or cut out a picture to refer to as you write your poems, or conjure up the person's image.

Sports

Throughout this book, I have used many sports allusions. Many great poems have a theme wrapped around sports. Have you read or heard "Casey at the Bat" yet? It's among my favorite poems. "Foul Shot" by Edwin A. Hoey, "The Base Stealer" by Robert Francis, and "The Fish" by Elizabeth Bishop, https://www.poemhunter.com/poem/the-fish/, have whet the interest of a few athletes in my class.

Since I played field hockey in college years ago, I chose to include a field hockey poem in my collection. After reading "Zoey Jubert," decide if it captures the mood of the final seconds of a tied game.

I challenge you to write a poem that enables the reader to share the excitement you felt at a particular moment in your favorite sport or game.

Louder Than a Shout, Softer Than a Whisper: Slam Poetry

It's the seventh-inning stretch. The poems are written. What's next? Ever heard "It ain't over till the fat lady sings"? The colloquialism, which probably originally referred to the stereotypical fat ladies of the opera, was made famous in our era by legendary baseball catcher and Hall of Famer, Yogi Berra.

Although not all poets want to publish their poems, poems lend themselves to being shared. Many people enjoy performing the poems they've written, more than writing them. Often the readings are in the form of slams and other competitions at cafés, libraries, and festivals, such as the Southern Fried Poetry Festival. Other readings are performed in high schools, colleges, and at open mic nights across the country, even in local bars like the Abbey in Downtown Deland, Florida, winner of America's 2017 Main Street.

No one wants to listen to someone mumble when reading. The time to strut your stuff approaches. Be a rooster. Know how to read your poems with the passion you felt when writing them.

Poetry should sound like its meaning. Let's go back to our baseball analogy. When we attend a baseball game, we don't have to hear the umpire's words to know if the pitch was a ball or a strike. Umpires say *Strike* in a long, loud, stretched-out voice. They say *Ball* in a lower voice—short and clipped. Additionally, they use specific hand motions to signify ball or strike.

Delivery is the use of voice and body to help convey the message of a poem. When slamming or reading poetry, pay attention to the message your body is sending the audience as well as to the words you are delivering.

Did you ever have a conversation with a parent that went something like this?

Mom: *Don't talk to me in that tone of voice.*

You: *What? I didn't say anything bad.*
Mom: *It isn't what you said. It's how you*
   said it. Don't use that tone with me.

There you have it. It isn't just what we say that counts in a poetry reading. It's how we present the material that allows us to convey meaning.

Have you ever heard of a pregnant pause? For a greater dramatic effect, sometimes a pause is better than a shout. It builds up suspense, getting the attention of the listener, and gives the impression that it will be followed by something significant. Other times it is used for comedic effect. Plan ahead for your delivery. Make every word, movement, and pause count.

Consider the following aspects of delivery when reading your own work or the work of others:

Techniques to Convey Meaning:

• *Use Accurate phrasing* to communicate meaning. Don't automatically pause at the end of a line. Pause at the end of a thought or to indicate something important is pending. Actors are often taught that Shakespeare's sonnets and plays are meant to be understood by pausing for punctuation, not line breaks or rhyme schemes. Practice taking a deep breath before reading poems without much punctuation.

• *Give Appropriate emphasis* to communicate meaning. One should almost lose words like *the*, but stress active verbs.

• *Establish* mood (tone), feeling, atmosphere.

• *Communicate the emotion* you intend to bring to mind. Sad, depressed, lighthearted? Think about how to say the words to convey the mood. How is your posture different when you are sad from when you just found out you're in the starting lineup? Body drooping or bouncy?

• *Communicate the climax or high poin*t. The poem should build to a crescendo. Then slowly return to your normal speaking voice.

• *Be enthusiastic*. Don't deliver your words as if you're waking up from a long nap. Let the listener know you care about the theme of your poem.

• *Connote or suggest the emotional intent* of the chosen words. As a poet, one chooses words for their implied meanings, not just the literal dictionary meanings. Read the words so your audience can tell the meaning of words by how you say them. Try this experiment. In a calm, tender voice, smile, pet your dog, and say, "Bad, bad dog." Does the dog wag or tuck its tail? It's how you say it, not what you say sometimes.

How are the emotions of the words *house* and *home* different? Why did poet Brewster Martin Higley VI and composer Daniel E. Kelley choose to name the poem and folk song "Home on the Range" rather than "House on the Range"?

• *Use Denotation properly*. It is as important as connotation. Check dictionary definitions of unfamiliar words. Use the proper word to safeguard against misunderstanding. Using concrete nouns allows your listeners to experience with one or more of their five senses. Abstract nouns like *love, patriotism*, and *beauty* are intangible. They mean different things to different people. Be careful about overusing them.

Body Movements

Do a quick check.

• Do your body actions coordinate with the thoughts and emotions the poem conveys?

• Do your facial expressions match the meaning of the words?

• Do you maintain eye contact with the audience?

Voice

The sound we produce is called **voice**.

The major characteristics of voice are:
- Pitch – The highness or lowness of voice.
- Volume – The loudness of the tone we make.
- Rate – The speed at which we talk.
- Quality, or tone, expresses personality and conveys emotion.

Quality is the tone, timbre, or sound of your voice. For example, voices are characterized as being clear, nasal, breathy, harsh, hoarse, piercing, ear splitting, or grating.

Avoid a monotonous voice characterized by pitch, volume, and rate remaining constant, without any word, phrase, or idea differing from any other.

Avoid a constant vocal pattern. Vocal variation should not be the same for every line or regardless of meaning. For example, don't end every line with an upward pitch or go up in the middle, or down at the end of every line.

Remember to avoid stopping at the end of lines unless there is a comma to indicate a slight pause, or a period to indicate a longer pause.

NOTE: If you are reading someone else's work, do you communicate the author's intended meaning?

Does your voice:

- *Demonstrate a pleasant, clear quality?*

- *Have the appropriate pitch level?* For normal conversation, a medium pitch produced by a relaxed throat is the most pleasant to hear and projects the farthest. In slamming or acting, use a high pitch to communicate excitement, anger, and shyness. Use a low pitch to express sadness, disgust, or despair.

• *Have the appropriate inflection?* Does your pitch rise for a question? Does your inflection or pitch fall to signify the end of a sentence or poem? To express doubt, innuendo, and sarcasm, do you combine rising and falling inflections?

• *Have adequate volume?*

• *Have the approriate rate?* Vary according to meaning. Young children speak faster than older people. The speed at which you talk suggests both age and emotion. Use a fast rate to indicate the emotions of happiness, excitement, and anger. Slow the speed at which you talk to suggest sorrow, doubt, thought, and respect.

• *Articulate clearly?* Open your mouth and enunciate. Don't let your voice trail off at the ends of words or sentences.

• Finally, be sure to *pronounce words carefully*. Refer to an online dictionary. For example, type in "how do I pronounce *enunciate*." Online dictionaries will pronounce the words for you. Select one.

Always Make Your Manuscript Easy to Read

Participants performing oral readings for many college forensic (speech) teams use small, black seven-and-a-half-inch by nine-inch three-ring binders so they can easily turn the pages when reading. Try their techniques to improve your slams.

When preparing a poem for oral reading or slamming, you might want to do the following:

- Triple-space. It helps you maintain eye contact without losing your place.

- Highlight the manuscript using different colors for different characters if there is dialogue.

- Use another color ink for narration.

- Write notes to yourself on the manuscript, such as *pause*, *speed up*, *read faster*, and *whisper*. Yes, whisper. It's possible to whisper loudly enough to be heard in the back of a room. Good vocal variety includes using a normal speaking voice and raising one's voice for emphasis, but sometimes it also requires lowering the voice to evoke or suggest meaning.

- To do the best job possible conveying your message, practice reading your poem with the prepared manuscript. Practice until you re able to maintain eye contact with your audience. When you are able to maintain eye contact for at least ninety percent of the time, you are ready to speak. Beware: Reading from a cellphone may result in delays or missed lines.

- Time your turning of the pages so there's no need to look down at your script while turning the manuscript. To convey the mood, avoid calling attention to the script. Keep the words and meaning in the minds of the listeners.

A Few Final Thoughts

Do what is necessary to prepare and be composed before stepping up to the microphone. Give yourself the proper equipment. Wear clothing that enables you to feel good about yourself. Consider wearing your favorite outfit or a traditional white blouse and black skirt or slacks. Avoid sweat pants. It's important not to call attention to your attire. Keep the poem foremost in the mind of the audience members.

Picture yourself delivering the poem perfectly. You know the nuances of your poem better than anyone else. It's your chance to be the hero or heroine of your own work.

The bases are loaded, with two outs, two strikes, and three balls in the bottom of the ninth. You're on the mound. Get the signal from the catcher (the introduction by the emcee). Take a deep breath. Get in the mood. (Don't giggle if it's a serious poem or frown if it's a humorous poem.) Use your voice and body to deliver the mood and message—your poem—with the game-winning pitch.

Game over! Game won. You are a poet.

SOURCES CONSULTED

Abbe, George. *Stephen Vincent Benét on Writing: Letters to a Young Beginning Author*. Brattleboro, VT: Stephen Greene Press, 1964.

Addonizio, Kim, and Laux, Dorianne. *The Poet's Companion: A Guide to the Pleasures of Writing Poetry*. New York: W.W. Norton & Company, 1997.

Finn, Louise. *Your Turn: 33 Lessons in Poetry*. Portland, ME: J Weston Walch, publisher, 1998.

King, Stephen. *On Writing: A Memoir of the Craft.* New York: Scribner, 2000.

Masters, Edgar Lee. *Spoon River Anthology.* New York: Macmillan Publishing Company, 1962.

Meinke, Peter. *The Shape of Poetry: A Practical Guide to Writing & Reading Poems.* Tampa, FL: University of Tampa Press, 2012. Padgett, Ron, ed. *Handbook of Poetic Forms*. New York: Teachers and Writers Collaborative, Second Edition, 2000.

Sims, Elizabeth. *You've Got a Book in You: A Stress-Free Guide to Writing the Book of Your Dreams.* Blue Ash: Writer's Digest Books, 2013.

Welty, Tara. "Taylor Swift: If you want to know what this singer is thinking, just listen to her songs," *Scholastic Action*, February 22, 2010.

From hubpages.com

Hayden, Robert. "The Whipping." *All Poetry*
https://allpoetry.com/The-Whipping

"Poetry is an echo, asking a shadow to dance." *Brainy Quote*. 12 Feb. *2018*. carl_sandburg_*107259*

Rothman, Joshua. "The Origins of Privilege. *The New Yorker* "May 12, 2914 https://www.newyorker.com/books/page-turner/the-origins-of-privilege

Von Goethe, Johann Wolfgang."Personality is everything in art and poetry."*Brainy Quote*. 12 Feb. *2018*. quotes johann_wolfgang_von_goethe_15052

About Melody

Melody taught at Northern Adirondack Central School and at the State University of New York at Plattsburgh. She draws from her teaching experiences to write Young Adult fiction and poetry. Her latest novel, *Blame*, was published by Taylor and Seale Publishing. Her short works appear in five Florida Writers Association (FWA) collections. Her *Backpack Blues* won a First-Place Royal Palm Literary Award (Unpublished General). "Ysobel Gomez," captured a Second Place award. She leads the FWA Villa Writers Group, belongs to the Society of Children's Book Writers and Illustrators (SCBWI) and spoke on a panel at the SCBWI Conference in Miami. Currently, Melody serves as president of the Florida Writers Foundation, Inc.

In her spare time, Melody loves to play pickleball with her husband, Barry, and pinochle with her son and his wife.

Other Books by Melody Dean Dimick:

Silent Screams
Sinister Silence
Blame

Short Works Published by Peppertree Press:

"Sorry"
"Ain't It a Shame"
"Come One, Come All"

Short Works Published by Black Oyster Publishing:

"Do Not Hide"
"Befriending Mabel"

Melody enjoys hearing from her readers. Go to her website:

http://www.melodydeandimick.com

Click *Contact Melody*.

CPSIA information can be obtained
at www.ICGtesting.com
Printed in the USA
FSHW01n0547040518
47783FS

9 781943 789832